Praise for Leor

The Barrum

The Barrumbi Kids is a remarkably assured and accomplished first novel ... Norrington is a gifted author, and *The Barrumbi Kids* makes an important contribution to Australian literature for young readers. – Judith Ridge, *Australian Book Review*

This novel has a fine, atmospheric sense of the tropics. It also teaches reconciliation without being in the least preachy. – Lucy Sussex, *The Age*

New writer Leonie Norrington's writing beautifully evokes the people, sights, sounds and smells of [the Northern Territory]. She has a gift for taking readers inside her characters – to understand what's important to them: the land and its people. – Jane Watson-Brown, *Australian Bookseller and Publisher*

The story is always lively, full of incidents and interactions which will interest all children and spark the joy of recognition in those familiar with the environment and lifestyle. – Lyn Linning, *Magpies*

Short-listed in 2003 for the Children's Book Council of Australia's Book of the Year (Younger Readers) Award, and for the New South Wales Premier's Literary Awards.

The Spirit of Barrumbi

Leonie Norrington

To dear Sally
For mateship
and Country
love
Leonie

An Omnibus Book from Scholastic Australia

LEXILE™ 690

Omnibus Books
175–177Young Street, Parkside SA 5063
an imprint of Scholastic Australia Pty Ltd (ABN 11 000 614 577)
PO Box 579, Gosford NSW 2250.
www.scholastic.com.au

Part of the Scholastic Group
Sydney • Auckland • New York • Toronto • London • Mexico City •
New Delhi • Hong Kong • Buenos Aires • Puerto Rico

First published in 2003.
Reprinted in 2004, 2008, 2010 (twice), 2013.

National Library of Australia Cataloguing-in-Publication entry

Norrington, Leonie.
The spirit of Barrumbi.
ISBN-13: 978 1 86291 552 7.
ISBN-10: 1 86291 552 0.
1. Aborigines, Australian – Northern Territory – Juvenile fiction.
2. Culture conflict – Juvenile fiction. 3. Floods – Juvenile fiction.
I. Title.
A823.3

Typeset in 13/15 pt Perpetua by Clinton Ellicott, Adelaide.
Printed and bound by McPherson's Printing Group, Victoria.
Scholastic Australia's policy, in association with McPherson's Printing Group, is to use papers that are renewable and made efficiently from wood grown in sustainable forests, so as to minimise its environmental footprint.

10 9 8 7 6 13 14 15 16 17 18 19 20/ 0

Dedicated to my dad,
who tried against all odds to keep us safe

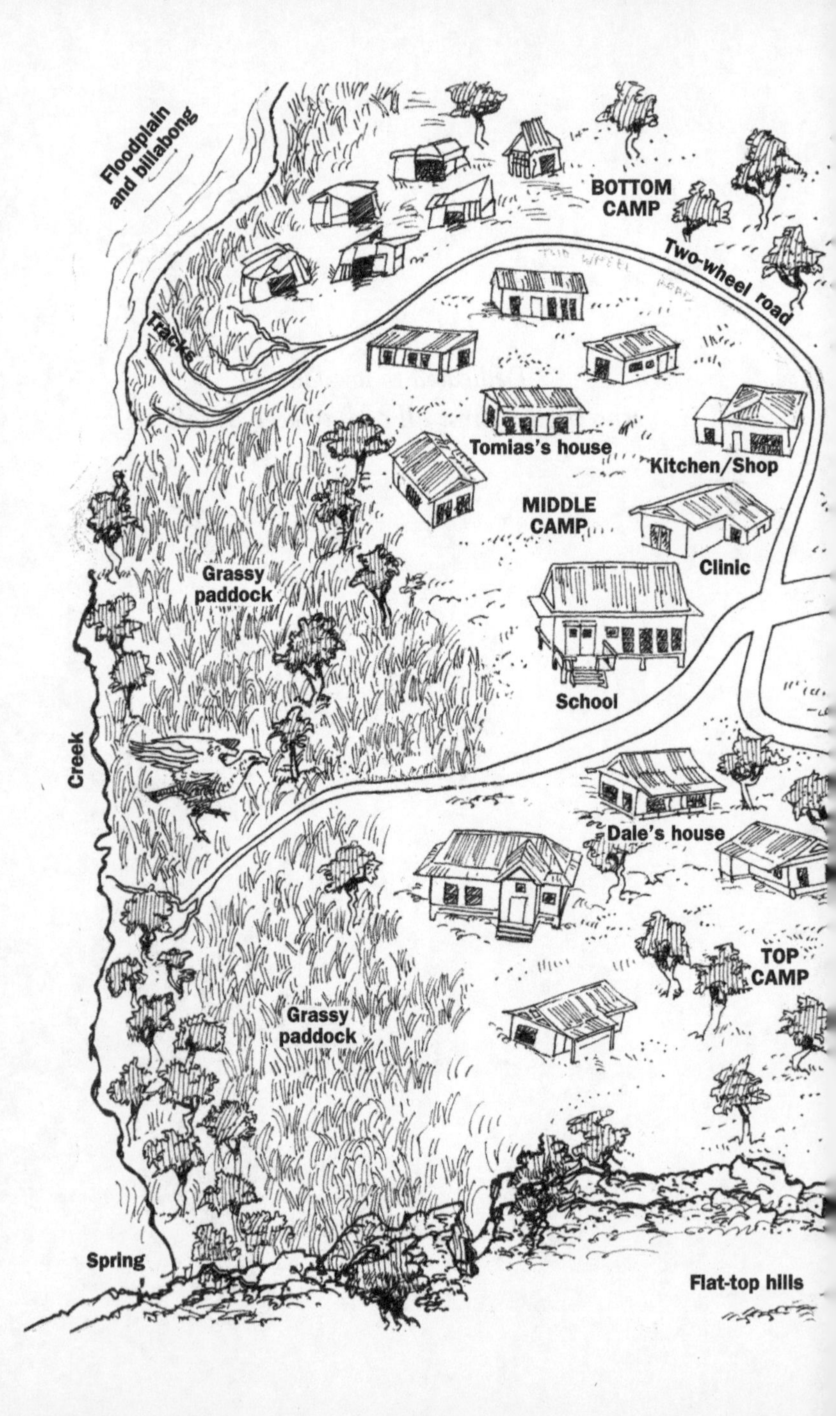
Floodplain and billabong
BOTTOM CAMP
Two-wheel road
Tracks
Tomias's house
Kitchen/Shop
MIDDLE CAMP
Clinic
Grassy paddock
School
Creek
Dale's house
TOP CAMP
Grassy paddock
Spring
Flat-top hills

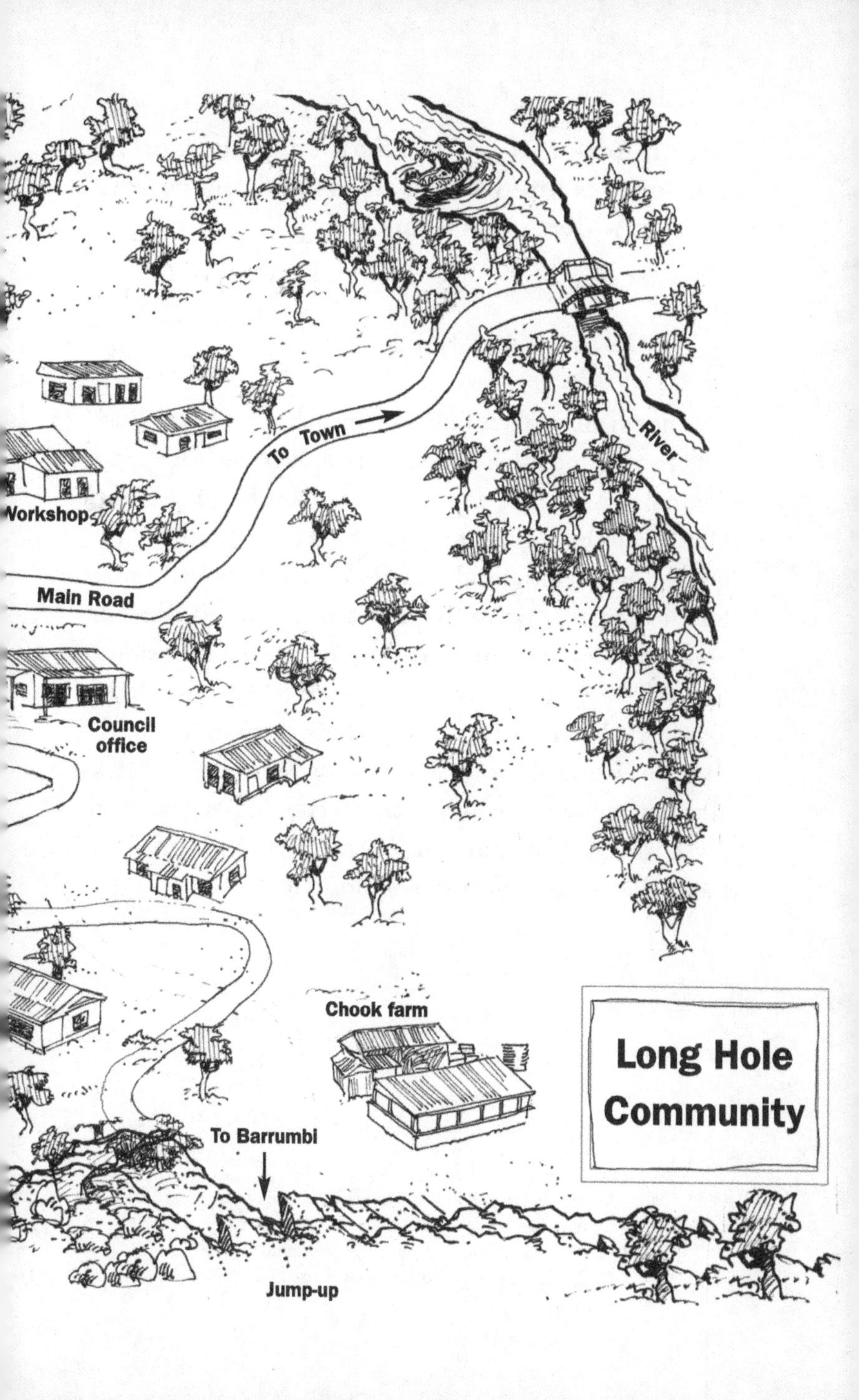

To Town
River
Workshop
Main Road
Council office
Chook farm
Long Hole Community
To Barrumbi
Jump-up

'Death Adder Ridge' is a fictional place, and no reference is intended to any specific place with 'Death Adder' in its name. – L.N.

Acknowledgments

The north Australian bush for inspiration. Clare Bush for growing me up. Old Mayali people from Wuggularr community for allowing me to use their language. Kim Caraher for her brilliant mentoring. Penny Matthews for her clever and insightful editing. Varuna Writers Centre for the place to write the first draft. Wilfred Russell-Smith for reading and commenting on the first draft. Philomena van Rijswijk for Sir Galahad. Northern Territory Writers Centre for their ongoing support. Australia Council for the Developing Writers grant that allowed me time to write and write and write. And my husband Alan and sons Shane, Kris and Luke for their insights into what blokes don't do.

In writing this book, the author was assisted by a Developing Writers grant from the Literature Board of the Australia Council, the Federal Government's arts funding and advisory body.

Contents

1

Barrumbi

Dale's biggest brother Sean is walking along the high escarpment holding an egg carton. He jumps from rock to rock, avoiding the spiky clumps of spinifex. Their yellow seeds rattle softly in the breeze. Tiny lights sparkle on the rocks in the hot sun. Behind him the sky is blue, blue as blue, and empty. It's late Dry season time. The world is still, waiting for the rain.

Inside the egg carton a tiny snake coils around itself. Its stumpy tail flickers. The triangle markings along its back disguise it in the uneven darkness.

Sean smiles, and stops to check his new possession. He opens the lid. The little snake stands up, its body curled beneath it, head high and back, fangs out, ready to strike. It's a baby death adder – only tiny, but already it has enough poison in its fang sacs to kill Sean.

'Wicked,' Sean says, closing the lid and walking again.

He's been to Death Adder Ridge. He's not allowed there. That's a sacred place. Not even the old men go there. He doesn't care! He thinks it's okay because nobody saw him.

Sean slows down, stops, crouches.

He's going to let the little snake go. Yes! He's not going to take it home.

As the lid opens the little snake rears up into striking position. It slips out of the egg carton and along the flat rock, looking for a place to hide.

Swoosh! Crack! A flash of blue, a snap of wings, and it's gone. Gone!

What? Sean stares in disbelief.

A kookaburra flaps up to a branch, whacks the little snake *slap, slap* near his feet, lifts his head back, and with a couple of gulps swallows it whole.

Slowly a sound comes up out of the ground – a slow vibration at first, not like a sound at all. It gets faster and faster till it becomes a humming, then louder and louder, filling his ears, bouncing off his chest, making his eardrums sting.

There's a shadow behind him, a huge dark cloud, loose like smoke. But it doesn't drift away; it tightens, rising up tall and thin. It draws back into an S shape. It's a snake! A death adder! Its head flattens into a hood, eyes glow red, and *whip!* it strikes, curved fangs stabbing right through Sean's neck. His body stretches up in pain. His mouth opens in a scream.

'Ahhh!' Dale screams and sits up.

Black. Everything's black. Stars sparkle in black sky.

'A dream. It's just a dream,' he whispers to himself, his body prickling with fear. We're camping. Remember? Camping at Barrumbi. There's Sean there, asleep in his swag by his fire. There's Mum and Dad, their mozzie net hanging pale from a tree. There's sister Lizzie and brother Jimmy's swags, and there's big sister Megan with her best friend Jeweleen. Everyone's okay.

Dale shivers. The sweat on his skin is cold. He lies

back down in his swag, pulling the sheet up to his chin. *Remember, the rain was late? That's why we had to come to Barrumbi.*

In his mind he sees his home at Long Hole community, the white-hot glare bouncing up from the tin roofs, the pale skies of the late Dry season staying above them for months and months until there's no water anywhere. Even the big river has dried up to shallow green pools, their surface covered with dry leaves.

The old people said it had never been this dry before. So the old lady Caroleena made them come to Barrumbi to do ceremony. To make the rain come. This is what they did in the old days. Every year the people came here to Barrumbi, to the deep waterhole hidden up in the hot dry escarpment between two sheer cliffs of stone, because the country needs children. Children playing and yelling out, their feet stamping on the ground. It needs their voices to wake it up, so it knows that the people are still here. That the people still belong. And then the rain will come.

The night is dark and quiet. The old people have stopped singing. Dale rolls over to look. There's the old men's camp by the truck. All through the night they and Caroleena were singing – not real corroboree, just singing up the country. Singing for the rain. Dale could feel the spirits moving through the air, skipping up the rocks and round the camp. He kept his eyes closed so he wouldn't accidentally see one, but he couldn't get to sleep. He just kept thinking and worrying.

Now the old people are silent. The ceremony's over.

Dale lies on his back. Millions of stars hang in the air. There's still no clouds in the sky. Nothing has changed. What if the ceremony doesn't work? What if the rains never come again?

Beside him Dale hears his best friend Tomias breathing in his swag.

He rolls over. 'Tomias?'

No answer.

Dale rolls back again, looking at the camp. He props himself up on his elbows, holding his hair back off his face: it's like a brown mop, always in his eyes. In the firelight he sees the main camp asleep. There's Caroleena, her huge bulk in the centre of the communal tarp, all the little kids around her and a ring of small mozzie fires around them. Since Dale was a little boy, Caroleena's serious face and her deep knowledge of the world made him feel warm and secure. And Tomias's mum Mavis too. Mavis and Dale's mum Lucy grew up together. They call each other sister. Dale and his brothers and sisters call Mavis auntie. She teaches them about bushtucker, law, and proper behaviour. She's like another mother for Dale. Better than a mother really, 'cause she'll stick up for him even if he's done something wrong. Not like his own mum.

Tomias snorts and rolls over in his sleep.

'Tomias,' Dale whispers again.

No answer.

Bloody Tomias. Dale smiles, shaking his head as he lies down again. Tomias could sleep through anything. He's so cool. He's really good at sport, and clever. Everyone likes him. He's Dale's best mate. No, more than that. Tomias is Dale's brother, his cousin brother. They have known each other all their lives – thirteen, nearly fourteen years. No, longer. When Mum and Mavis were pregnant they sat together, their bare hands in the dirt so that the babies inside them could listen to the talk and feel their country beneath them. So, in a way, Dale and Tomias knew each other even before they were born.

A couple of metres away Dale's biggest brother Sean lies in his swag, not daring to move. What the hell's Dale doing awake! he thinks. Last thing I need today is Dale following me or telling anyone where I've gone. He's probably having bad dreams. He's such a scaredy cat. I'll have to wait now till he goes back to sleep.

The moon hangs full in the west; the faint grey of morning lights up the sky in the east. The first flying foxes are coming home, chattering, arguing, trying to find their babies in the nursery. It must be about five o'clock.

Sean woke up throughout the night, checking the time by the moon and the animals. He has a lot of knowledge already. His family's lived here with the Aboriginal people for three generations. Sean's grandfather moved into this country to build a cattle station. His mother grew up with Mavis, so she knows about bushtucker and the land. Mavis taught Sean when he was young, and now the men are teaching him.

Isn't it strange, Sean thinks, that the old men should spend all night singing for rain. These old men know everything about the natural world, everything. They can name every plant and animal. They know when the insects, birds and animals are mating and ready to give birth; when the food animals are fat and ready to eat; when the trees are going to flower. Yet they think they can change the weather by singing.

A quoll comes running along the edge of the camp, growling and complaining to itself, the white spots along its back illuminated in the darkness. Djabbo – northern quoll – *Dasyurus halucatus*, Sean thinks. It's coming back from a night's hunting – must be close to five-thirty. I'll have to go soon.

Dale rolls over and back again.

Go to sleep, you little mongrel, Sean thinks.

At first Sean didn't want to come to Barrumbi, to waste his holidays camping with the family. He wanted to go hunting, fishing and collecting snakes by himself or with his friends.

Then one night he saw Barrumbi on a map, and realised it was only a couple of hours' walk from Death Adder Ridge – home to a large colony of northern death adders. Death Adder Ridge! He remembered Mavis warning him about it when he was little. 'Don't you go that place. Spirit there,' she said, her eyes dark and serious. 'No one comes back from that place. Even that clever old man don't go there.'

When Sean was little, he believed her. But not any more. The only reason he hasn't been to Death Adder Ridge before is that it's two days' walk from home.

Now he's here at Barrumbi and it's morning and he can't believe his luck. Today, this day now, he's going to Death Adder Ridge. All he has to do is get out of camp without anyone seeing, and in a couple of hours he'll be at Death Adder Ridge. This time of year, when it's hot and humid, death adders are active – coming out to find mates, giving birth to a tangling mess of live babies. There'll be heaps of them out there. He'll definitely get a death adder today!

While he waits, Sean checks his first-aid equipment in his mind. Snake bandages, silver thermal blanket, water, dried food, compass, knife, needle. The bush isn't dangerous if you're prepared.

Dale has been silent for the last half hour. Better go, Sean thinks. He puts on his boots, grabs his backpack and walks out of the camp in the eerie grey light.

Dale lies awake. He hears his brother get up. Sean must be going hunting for snakes, he thinks. I should tell him about the dream! Quickly he rolls over to yell out to Sean. But Sean is already near Mavis, his silhouette walking carefully over bodies and around blankets.

Dale stops himself. No. Better not. He'll get really wild and reckon I'm a stupid wussy wuss. Sean wouldn't go near Death Adder Ridge. He'd never be that stupid. Sean is clever, brave. He knows language. He goes hunting with the men!

Now that the old men have stopped singing, Dale feels the earth become quiet and calm. He relaxes. As the sky lightens and the little escarpment finches wake up, squeaking and fluttering through the grass to their nests in the pandanus, he falls asleep.

2
A Scientific View

Sean walks along the high escarpment, stepping from rock to rock. Spiky clumps of spinifex prick his legs as he passes. The sun picks up tiny lights sparkling in the rocks. That's mica, he thinks. This rock was laid down millions of years ago. Layer on layer of silt and stone cemented together by great pressure. He jumps from rock to rock, avoiding the spinifex. Its yellow seeds rattle softly in the breeze.

Behind him the sky is blue, blue as blue, and empty. It's late Dry season time. The world is still, waiting for the rain.

Sean wants to work with snakes when he grows up. He found a clutch of snake eggs once, and took some home. Within half an hour of hatching, the baby snakes could strike and kill little frogs. He wrote this down in his notebook. Of all the animals in the world, Sean loves snakes best. He loves their smooth skin, the quick flicker of their tongues, the dark stillness of their eyes. He loves the feel of their muscles as they move across his hands. He has pythons and freshwater snakes in a terrarium in his bedroom, the bedroom he shares with his little brothers Dale and Jimmy. He feeds the snakes mice and small frogs, and watches the silent strike, the swift coils wrapping and tightening; the deliberate way the snake positions itself and swallows its prey whole, sliding its lips over the body, dislocating its jaw.

Last term, when Sean was at boarding school, he did work experience at the wildlife park and got to work with poisonous snakes – taipans, western browns, death adders. It was wicked! He could watch them for hours. Silent death. Instant death. So dangerous! He'd drop the mouse into the cage, sit down, and watch.

It knows. As soon as it falls into the snake cage, the little mouse knows. Its eyes widen with fear. It sniffs the air, whiskers twitching. It runs in panic – sometimes running right over the snake as it tries to get away. But the death adder waits. At the other end of the cage it's still, absolutely still. Its dark, empty eyes reflect the mouse's movements like a rock pool.

The mouse stops. Is it okay? Maybe it will be okay. It can smell danger but nothing's happening. It sits still, panic slowing draining from its eyes.

Whack!

Like an arrow the snake dives through the air, mouth open, fangs out.

Sean tries to watch, tries to keep his eyes open, but each time the snake strikes he blinks and misses the impact. A half-second blink, and the mouse is already jerking, poison pumping through its body. A minute later it's dead.

Sean's up on Death Adder Ridge now, looking for a crack in the escarpment. There's a crack about here that opens out to a deep ravine – very hard to see. Inside it, a tiny spring-fed creek, dark with leaf litter, feeds a huge rainforest. That's the only way you know it's there, the men say. As you walk along Death Adder Ridge you'll see the dark green leaves of the rainforest trees and know to keep away.

But there's nothing! Everything's pale green or grey – even the new leaves that emerged a few weeks ago, anticipating the rain, are drooping pale green.

Surely it's not the wrong ridge.

Sean stops and looks out to the horizon. 'There's Barrumbi up there.'

He pulls out his map. Is this the right place?

Yeah! Must be!

He looks carefully, holding the map up and checking it centimetre by centimetre against the landforms around him.

The ravine should be just there on the left.

Then he sees a long, thin spike – a palm frond spike.

'That's it.' He walks forward. 'That's got to be it. Palms don't grow on escarpments. They live in watered, sheltered places.'

The palm frond is not the right colour. Instead of being dark green it's pale grey, but the shape is right. It's definitely a palm frond.

He runs over and there it is – a crack in the rock, only fifteen centimetres wide and opening out into a gully. He couldn't see it because all the rainforest trees have lost their leaves. From the distance the tops emerging from the crack look like dead shrubs. But now he can see that this is it, definitely. He runs along the edge of the gully.

The trunks of palm trees drop down, down into the

ravine. *Got to get down there.* He reaches for one of the trunks but it's too far away and he nearly falls in. Careful! Blood tingles through his body. 'Hurt yourself up here, mate, and you'll be long dead before anyone finds you,' he tells himself.

He walks along farther, but there's nowhere safe to climb down. The walls are smooth and steep, the trees just too far from the edge.

What's that up there? A banyan. The bare skeleton of a banyan fig, its new leaves wilted and fallen, its trunk melted against the cliff. It holds onto the rocky wall, filling cracks and crevices like candle wax, sending thick stilt-like trunks out and down into the ravine. Solid roots and branches to hold and stand on.

Sean climbs out onto the tree and slides down one of the trunks, *loose – grip, loose – grip*, as if he's sliding down a fireman's pole – swift, efficient and strong.

'Greenants!' He jumps to the ground, carefully wiping ants from his arms, his legs. Pulls off his backpack and shirt to find them in his armpits and elbow creases, their little mouths clamped tight, their green bums folded down upon themselves with the strain. His skin lifts up as he tries to pull them off without hurting or killing them. It's nearly impossible. Silly little buggers, he thinks.

The ground is soft, dry leaves crunch beneath his feet, the smell of moisture and compost is thick in his nostrils. No water. Dark. The sun never hits the ground just here. Around him tall trunks climb straight up. Basket ferns, dry and brown, cling to the red rock walls.

As he walks down, the gully widens into a deep sunlit

ravine. At the bottom there's a tiny creek overgrown with trees. On either side of it are open slopes of sand and rock. Above them walls of stone reach into the sky. Sean stays half way up the bank, climbing over the tumble of rocks that have fallen in slabs from the cliffs of yellow and red above him.

The air is heavy.

Gravity is never so obvious, so clearly true, he thinks, as when you're beneath a wall of rock aching to fall.

Imagine being squashed under that! He looks up at the huge square blocks, some the size of a truck, the stress lines clear around them. There are yellow and black stains where the water has already found its way into the cracks, eroding, loosening.

One block has recently fallen, leaving split tree trunks still fresh, the sap dried into rivers of red crystals, thick and soft underneath. That's what the old people used to attach stone spearheads to the shafts, Sean thinks, picking the red gum from the bark. The colour's rich, like fresh blood.

There's a movement in the sky. A bird hovers near the opposite cliff – might be a nest up there. A hawk? I wonder if it's Sir Galahad?

Last holidays Sean got a little pink baby hawk fallen from its nest high in a gum tree. He'd read in one of his mother's old books about knights and lords who raised hawks for hunting. Sean called the little hawk Sir Galahad, after one of the knights, and fed it a mixture of meat minced up with feathers, bone and egg. The little hawk grew quickly. Soon he would take a whole dead mouse and tear it to pieces himself.

Sean threw him up into the air to teach him how to fly and, tempting him with bits of food, taught him to come back when he whistled. Sir Galahad flew away for miles, but he always returned. Sean made him a hood and a jess and he looked wicked, just like a hawk in the pictures in the book.

Sean tried to teach him to kill a mouse. He took him out on the lawn and let a mouse go, but Sir Galahad just watched it run away, a shocked expression on his face, cocking his head from side to side. He wouldn't eat anything that wasn't dead. That's when Dale and Tomias nicknamed him Sir Cowardhad.

One day Sean got really annoyed and threw a live mouse at him. 'You're useless!' he said. Sir Galahad jumped into the air, caught it – *crunch!* – killed it and ate it. Next day he swooped down and killed the mouse Sean let go on the grass. Two days later he flew away and never came back.

I wonder if that's him? Sean narrows his eyes against the glare – gets his little binoculars out to have a better look. No. It's a peregrine falcon. That's what the noblemen in England used for hunting, peregrine falcons. They're amazing! God, those things can fly. They can hit speeds of up to two hundred kilometres an hour, snatching other birds out of the air on the wing.

Sean stands still, watching, waiting, hoping for a bird to come along, hoping to see a kill. Imagine if you saw a peregrine falcon kill a bird on the wing – not in a nature documentary – in real life. It would be so wicked. He continues to walk along, his eyes alert, watching everything.

A rock wallaby stops. She hears someone walking. Her ears circle like radar to locate the intruder, and she moves quietly up to the safety of her hide.

Between the rocks, in a small hollow, fallen leaves lie criss-crossed, long and thin, making patterns of dots and dashes. Nestled in among the leaves, the triangle pattern on his skin camouflaging him exactly, a death adder waits, his dark tongue slipping out to test the air, to feel the moisture, to read the vibrations.

The vibrations say *heavy animal*, probably a human. Just one. Too big to eat. His tongue also tells him of panic. Bandicoots hiding, little lizards darting under rocks, broken branches, squashed leaves.

The death adder waits, his body flat and still. No one, nothing, scares him. His eyes search for the animal. Come on, he thinks. Have a go. Try and chase me away and we'll see what you get. His tongue flickers from the tiny gap at the front of his mouth. His fangs tingle with anticipation, ready to strike and kill.

High in a cave at the top of the gorge the old men sit. They too sense the intruder. One old man moves away from the tiny fire to peer out the opening. He stands there for a while, then looks back at the others.

What? another old man asks, lifting his head slightly and turning his hand over. He's the most important ceremony man, a lawman.

'Mightbe someone.'

'Whatkind?' the lawman asks, annoyed. He has come a long way, he and his wife. They've walked and walked, over the floodplains, through the woodland, up into the escarpment, to get here to help these people with their ceremony.

'No one's allowed to come this place,' he says in language. 'Who owns him?'

'For Lucy. Born here now. Daughter for that old man. Long time station time.'

'Should he know not to come to this place?' the lawman asks again in language.

The other old men nod, ashamed.

They look at each other, fear prickling inside them.

Calling for help from spirits is dangerous – everything must be done carefully, exactly – one small mistake can cause great offence, even death.

There are times when a person can go near sacred places and be forgiven, someone sick, or mad, or someone who doesn't know – if they're respectful. The spirit might trip them up, tickle them while they're climbing the wall and make them fall, or just give them a cold feeling. But this boy. This boy knows. He's old enough to do ceremony. He should have done his first ceremony.

The old men walk back to the fire in silence. What will happen?

They look at the ceremony man.

He looks at the fire, his eyes narrow with anger.

Sean climbs farther down, closer to the creek, where the fallen rocks have turned to gravel. It's a steep slope with small shrubs and loose sandy soil. He takes off his backpack and starts to look, carefully turning over large stones, one by one. At this time of day the baby death adders will be hiding beneath rocks or logs where they're safe from the birds that would drop from the sky and snatch them up.

The sun beats down on his back and sweat fills his eyes, but he's happy, really happy, confident that today he'll be the owner of a little death adder.

3

The Spirit of Barrumbi

Through the eyes of the peregrine falcon, the tongue of the death adder, the ears of the rock wallaby, the land watches Sean enter the ravine. He intrudes without identifying himself; he squashes a line of greenants as he slides down the banyan tree, leaving them half broken, screaming, glued to the trunk in their own blood, their legs twitching. He tramples a patch of moss, cracking the miniature pine trees, leaving their stems split and broken; he brushes aside a spider's web, breaking the golden threads, forcing the spider to run to safety.

Yesterday the children's footsteps, their shrill voices vibrating through the air from Barrumbi, woke the country from a long sleep. Good. Good. The people have come back. Life and joy, movement, laughter from across the valley. The world's as it should be. This is good, murmured the land.

Now a thump of boots vibrates the rocks, and echoes bounce from the cliff walls. *Thump, thump.* There's panic in the air. Rushing, hiding animals.

The land absorbs the tension, soaks up the fear and anger. Inside the rock, inside the soil, inside the trees, it stirs. Lifting, moving, swelling, slipping out as warm vapour through the cracks. Sucking up the panic, swallowing the tension. The air is suddenly thick and moist, tumbling, building, lifting, rising. It rushes up out of the gorge and into the open sky. Up, out into the surrounding landscape, boiling into thick black clouds, heavy with anger.

Sean's back is bent. Sweat drips into his eyes. He pulls off his hat to wipe his face. His blond hair is dark with sweat, sticking to his scalp. Then a wind whips past him. He lifts his face to accept its coolness. The smell of rain fills his nostrils with pleasure. The sweat on his skin dries, cooling him.

Rain, he thinks, standing and straightening, looking around him.

Dark clouds are descending into the ravine.

Raindrops start to fall, hitting the soft gravel slopes around him, making holes in the soil as the impact bounces the dirt up into the air.

It's going to rain!

CRACK! Lightning crackles across the sky – electricity lifts his hair.

'Shit!' He crouches down. Gonna get hit by lightning.

He's out in the open on the loose gravel slope. Run back to the rainforest? It would be safer there among the trees. No – too far. He's come too far – never make it back in time. What about under the overhang?

He looks up. The rocks above him are dripping, water seeping through the cracks, washing the soil from between them. They will fall. It's too dangerous up there.

He looks down. That tiny creek will be raging in no time – flash flood – get washed away. Got to go up and along. Perhaps there's a cave.

Yes! There's a tall cliff further down, a dark patch in the rock wall. Is it a cave? Please make it a cave.

CRACK! Lightning cuts across the sky again and rain buckets down. Huge raindrops sting Sean's back, smacking into the earth, splatting mud up his legs, into his boots.

Can't see! He holds his hands above his eyes. He grabs his backpack, puts it on and starts climbing up, towards the cliff and hopefully the cave.

But the water has smelt him. It wants him. It falls heavy and cold from the sky, splashing onto Sean's warm flesh, melting into his hair and clothes, mingling with his sweat, feeling muscle move over bone, blood pumping through veins. It slips away too fast, screaming, crying, still wanting his warmth. The falling rain tries to hang on, to drag it down, not to let go. It mixes with the loose soil and turns it to mud, slippery mud. The ground's sliding, pulling Sean down. He's on his hands and knees, his boots slipping, slipping. Roll over, sit down, spread your legs, dig your boot heels in.

Below him the little creek rages. Just minutes before it was crystal clear, hardly moving. Now it's a mass of boiling red water, smashing against rocks and tree trunks. He's sliding towards it. He pulls his boots off – bare feet will give better grip. He rolls onto his stomach. His toes and fingernails bury themselves like claws in the mud. His abandoned boots sit for a moment beside him. They begin to slide, slowly at first, then more quickly as the muddy water gathers them up, rolling down the slope until *splash!* they go into the creek and disappear. One surfaces farther down, its blackness briefly visible in the boiling red water, then it's gone.

Sean is on his hands and knees. Thunder rumbles around him, rain pounds his back. He climbs over the rock and reaches for the next, pulling himself up to find another stronghold. He's got to go up and right. The cave's his only chance. He's moving quickly now, checking each hold before he trusts it. As long as he keeps moving, the water can't take hold of him, pull him down. He can't see more than a metre in front of him, but he knows he's going in the right direction, up and right. Up and right. The ground's like a muddy floodplain, a moving mass of water.

The water falls on the hot rocks of the escarpment, sizzling, becoming warm, slipping down between the cracks, over the moss and lichen, dissolving the bonds that hold them in place, melting into the rock, making it dark and heavy. Come down, it says, come down. Down.

Sean climbs and climbs, keeping his eyes closed against the mud and rain. At first the deep rumbling sound doesn't register in his brain. But then he feels it. Feels the ground shaking beneath his hands.

Crash! Rumble!

It's rocks falling! Even with his watery vision he can see the black mass coming down the slope. Quick! Roll! Roll! He lifts his hands above his head and rolls over and over, keeping his body vertical and rolling across the vibrating ground till he smacks into a deep-bedded rock. He crawls around it quickly, tucking his head into his legs, and the dark mass rumbles past, sending ripples through the sodden earth.

Safe.

But the water slides around the rock now, digging the dirt from under him.

His exhausted hands grab at the rock, but its smooth wet surface lets him go. He's floating, down, down, floating on a river of mud.

Then sharp rocks scrape against his toes, take skin off his shins, scratch hard along his stomach, bump into his chin.

His fingers clutch at the edge as he goes over.

Hanging. He's hanging over a cliff.

Water pours onto his face, filling his mouth, his eyes with mud. He can't breathe, his fingers weaken, slipping. Every ounce of energy in his body is in the ends of his fingers. Then something smashes down on them. Pain screeches through his body like an electric shock. A dark shape bounces over him. 'Ahhhh!' He's falling.

He lands on his feet, on a little ledge. On his hands and knees, crawling. His body's shaking so much his arms keep collapsing. A recess. Snuggled in against the wall, he hugs himself to hold his body still. His fingers are bleeding, swollen thick and blue where they were crushed against rock. One fingernail stands straight up; underneath, the flesh is puffed up, red raw, bloody. It's stinging, throbbing in the air.

Get bandages, cover up, stop infection.

He wriggles out of the soaking backpack, shoulders jittering, insides shaking, fingers screaming with pain.

'Get that first-aid blanket on. You're in shock,' he says to himself. 'You need to get warm.' He unwraps the tiny square of silver, using teeth and feet, wincing each time he moves his fingers. It opens out to a thin sheet and he pulls it crackling around his shoulders.

'You'll be right,' he says aloud. 'You've got everything you need in your backpack. The water won't come up this high. Just get warm, put some iodine on those fingers so they don't get infected and you'll be right. Panicking is what kills people!'

His fingers, yellow with iodine, are wrapped in the snake bandage. Still the rain pours down, but it can't get him now. The wind blows clouds of fine droplets onto his face. Against the rock he is safe and protected, warm. He pulls the first-aid blanket closer around himself, then he closes his eyes and leans back against the wall.

Suddenly he wakes with a jolt – the smash of rock on his fingernails – the burst of pain rushing through his body – his fingers crushed and bloodied – slipping, slipping! Then he feels the rock beneath him. 'It's okay. You're safe.' He stretches his hands out on the rock wall, holding onto its heat, trying to stay awake.

The rain falls, no wind, no thunder, just a heavy screen of grey water falling, falling from the sky.

Hungry. Need something sweet. Dried banana in the backpack. Hands gloved in bandages, clumsy, slowly find the food. Groans escape against his will from his mouth and he feels ashamed. Finally the sweet softness between his teeth warms and quietens his jittery belly and his fingers can rest.

Have to ration the food. This rain looks like it's setting in. Could be here for days.

Another fine gust of rain floats over him, leaving his face wet and cold. Should find a better place to hole up. He slips his backpack over one leg and, centimetre by centimetre, his broken hands jarring, he crawls painfully around the ledge, dragging the backpack behind him.

There's a small recess. Might be a cave.

Smoke! A fire!

The old men.

Sean quickly jumps back behind the wall so they won't see him – so quick his foot kicks the backpack to the edge.

He lunges forward to grab it before it topples over. But he's too late. It falls as if in slow motion, bouncing once, is still for a moment on the dirt, then the water running down the slope gathers it up and carries it rolling down to the creek.

'No!' Sean yells.

He hears his voice echo through the ravine and remembers the old men in the cave.

They look at him, then turn back to the fire.

Sean knows them. They're his teachers, his fathers.

They're sitting in a tight circle, their backs a solid wall – they don't move to give him space.

Sean crawls backwards around the corner, back to his place against the wall, pulling his crinkly blanket around him.

He's been caught. Caught in this illegal place. A hot flush of shame, guilt and dread spreads through his body. Then fear. What will they do?

This is bad. Really bad. They might kill me. As soon as the rain stops I've got to get away. They are going to be really pissed off.

A greenant bites the inside of his leg.

'Bastard!' Sean says, squashing it fiercely through his pants.

4

Getting Turtle

The women are out on the floodplain when the storm hits, hunting for turtle. Tomias's mum Mavis and old Caroleena walk in front, their brightly coloured dresses swaying around their legs. Dale's mum carries his littlest sister Susan on her hip, her body in a curve pushing her hip out, her wide-brimmed hat shading her face, her long red plait down her back. Lizzie carries Tomias's little brother Alfred up on her shoulders. He holds tight to her red pigtails sticking out of the holes she cut in the sides of her hat. Lizzie wears the weirdest fashions. She even wears dresses over her jeans.

The little kids run around playing in between legs, teasing each other, ducking behind skirts and pulling at them as they hide.

'Look out you mob,' Lizzie yells as her little brother Leroy swings around her, nearly pulling her over. 'Get out!' She bites her turned-over tongue, gammon real angry, lifting her hand to smack him.

He covers his head and runs away to snuggle against Caroleena's leg, peeking out at Lizzie to see if she's really angry. His blue eyes are wide in his dirty little face.

Caroleena laughs at Leroy, his face so serious. She pulls him close. 'She big cranky one that Lizzie, na

Leroy,' she says. 'Not you hey. You good boy, hey.' Her huge body wobbles with laughing.

'Yeah,' Leroy says, sticking his tongue out at Lizzie.

Lizzie scowls an *I'll get you later* scowl. She pulls Alfred down from her shoulders, kisses his face. 'You good boy hey Alfred, not Leroy. He's too cheeky hey.'

Mavis, Caroleena, Jeweleen and Meg carry their digging sticks – thin pieces of steel bar. Caroleena's dilly bag hangs down her broad back, its band around her forehead. She has already got one turtle. She holds it by the neck and lets its body hang in the folds of her skirt.

'That's how come he got long neck, that gomrdau,' Lizzie says, and Meg and Jeweleen laugh.

'Don't you make that joke.' Caroleena scowls at them. 'Him live. He listen you cheeky one.'

Leroy smiles because now Lizzie's in trouble. He tries to catch her eye to tease her but she ignores him.

It was just a joke, Lizzie thinks. Can't ya joke about anything around here? She looks quickly at Mum. Whew, glad Mum didn't hear. Mum always takes Caroleena's side. Lizzie looks at Mavis to see if she will stick up for her, but Mavis is talking to Meg. Lizzie lifts Alfred up onto her shoulders again and walks off. Bloody Meg, she gets everything. Just because she's older than me she gets to go hunting and learn stuff. It's a waste of time. Meg can't remember a thing. All she's interested in is books and clothes and hairdos.

'You subbie gomrdau?' Mavis asks Meg. Then, seeing Meg struggle to remember, she says, 'Long-neck turtle, gomrdau.'

Meg nods. Gomrdau is connected to the Rainbow Serpent somehow, she remembers, but how? She'd better not ask. Mavis will growl her. She's supposed to remember, but when she goes away to boarding school she forgets everything. She walks along, lifting and pushing her crowbar into the soil, scanning the ground for any sign of turtle. She's hot. She wears a long-sleeved shirt and a big wide-brimmed hat to stop the sun burning her skin and making new freckles, but still she's hot. She hates her freckles. She wants to have smooth skin like Jeweleen's, smooth and black. Even smooth and white would be better than all spotty and red!

Meg and Jeweleen are best friends. They're fifteen. Ready, Mavis reckons, to learn to be women. So when Meg comes home from boarding school Mavis takes her and Jeweleen out with the old women. The women look at their little breasts pushing their shirts out and sigh, nodding – yes, this is the right time for them. They talk with them about grown-up gossip and try to separate them from Lizzie and the other little girls. Although they all know that Meg will never learn as fast as Lizzie, they're teaching her how to hunt turtle with Jeweleen and leaving Lizzie to look after little Alfred.

At this time of year there's no water anywhere. The string of billabongs is completely dried out, leaving a blacksoil plain cracked into scaly patterns. As the water in the billabongs dries up, turtles settle themselves down into the soft mud, keeping a breathing hole open with their breath. The sun bakes the surface hard as concrete, trapping them in their moist caverns, where they survive until the rains come.

Maybe that's the connection to the Rainbow Serpent, Meg thinks. Maybe it's to do with them burying themselves in the ground. I'll ask Lizzie later. Lizzie always remembers.

Meg's arms are tired. The ground is hard and it's not easy to push the digging stick through the baked crust. Blisters are starting on her palms. She thinks about what Mum said, about how turtles slow their heartbeat down and take shallow breaths when they're under the ground to conserve their energy. They sort of go to sleep so they can stay alive for months without eating or drinking. Mum reckons that humans can do it too. She reckons that in India holy men slow their bodies down so much they don't feel pain or hunger. They do it with their breathing. They breathe real slow and stop their minds from thinking and worrying. They keep their bodies still so they don't use energy. Mum tried to show her how to do it. They sat down together and breathed. 'Count to ten while you breathe in. Take the breath right down into your stomach. Follow it with your mind and then let it out, counting to ten,' Mum told her.

'I can't do it. I run out of air.'

'You'll be able to if you practise. Just concentrate on breathing and let the thoughts flow through your mind.'

'I can't stop thinking.'

'You don't have to stop. Just don't take any notice of your thoughts and they'll go away.'

How wonderful it would be, Meg thinks now on the floodplain, to be able to do that breathing. To get away from the hassle of having to learn, the noise and chatter of family, Mavis and Caroleena's expectations, school. At school she sleeps in a dormitory with ten other girls. Even at home she has to share her bedroom – the girls' room – with Lizzie, and little Susan will come in when she's old enough. If she could do this breathing she could make her own silence, not worry about school or Mavis or anything. But she can't. She's tried and tried, practised and practised. She got a bit better, but she never got it right. There was always something to worry about.

Hey, she thinks now. How come I can remember all that stuff about breathing but not the name of the long-neck turtle. What was it? I've forgotten it again. She walks over to her mum. 'Mum, what's the long-neck turtle's name?'

'Gomrdau.'

'That's right, gomrdau,' Meg says. 'Gomrdau. Gomrdau. I wonder if that gomrdau can hear us, if they're worried about getting eaten. Do you think they worry and use up more energy?'

'I suppose they do.'

'Don't you worry about me,' Meg says out loud to the turtles. 'I'll never find you. I'm hopeless.'

'Just relax,' Mum says. 'Just relax and let your body direct you. The knowledge is there inside you. Just relax and let it out.'

Right! Meg thinks. She knows what she's supposed to do. She knows to look for the turtle's breathing hole. When you find it you push the crowbar into the soil to tap on its shell, listening to hear the clunk and the soft sigh. Then you dig him up with your crowbar.

But how? How do you know where to look? She doesn't ask. She knows what they'll say. 'You watch.' But she *does* watch. Mavis and Caroleena are directed by magic. They just know where to look. Even Jeweleen knows.

'Just let your eyes scan the surface and you'll see it,' Mum says, stopping to give little Susan a drink from her backpack.

Megan tries. She lets her mind go free and relaxes, scanning the soil for that breathing hole, moving away from Mum and back to the other women. But all the crevices look the same, except ... Does that one have more loose dirt around it?

She pushes the crowbar in. *Clunk!*

'Oh yes!' she says.

Mavis, Caroleena and Jeweleen walk on.

I'll show them, Meg thinks. She squats down, tucking her skirt between her legs and digging quickly with her crowbar.

Lizzie and the kids stop to watch her. 'You got turtle Meg?' they ask.

She keeps digging, two hands on the stick, jabbing it into the ground to break it up and then pulling the soil out with her cupped hands. She can see the shell and stabs the crowbar underneath it to lift it up.

But it's just a rock.

Meg gets up. 'It's no use!' she says. The sun's hot – stinking hot – burning her skin. She can feel her face all red and flustered, more freckles erupting like pimples. On the horizon the line of trees shimmers grey and green in the heat. She narrows her eyes to the glare and watches the clouds brewing in the distance. They move quickly, rolling over themselves.

'It might rain!' she yells, and looks around for the others. Jeweleen's close by. Caroleena and Mavis are a little way off, Mum farther still. Their long bodies seem to be floating, their bright yellow and red dresses shimmer in the heat. Lizzie and the little kids are watching the clouds – dark and threatening underneath, pure white on top – as they roll across the sky. The floodplain stretches out wide beneath them.

'Mightbe big storm,' Meg yells out to the others. She wants to go back to the camp.

Mavis looks up and lifts her hand to say, Don't talk about it. Just wait and see if the rain comes.

'Meg, good girl,' Caroleena yells out.

Oh, what now? Meg thinks. What have I done now? I can never get anything right. They expect me to know everything.

She walks over to where Caroleena and Mavis are standing.

Caroleena points to the ground with her lips. 'Mightbe gomrdau,' she says.

Meg looks. 'Where?'

Caroleena waits.

Meg sits down and looks closely.

Caroleena pokes near the hole with her crowbar.

'Oh, there.' It's no different from any other crack in the blacksoil, except it looks used somehow. Yes, it's used. That's it. That's the way to tell. That's what you have to look for. Suddenly Meg knows and her face nearly breaks in half trying to stop smiling. She stands and presses her crowbar through the hard soil. *Clunk!* Was that a sigh? She looks at Caroleena.

Caroleena nods. Poor thing, she thinks, this little girl. How will she find a husband?

Mavis stops and looks up, comes over.

Meg starts digging one side, Mavis the other.

'See, look, Megan find turtle!' Caroleena yells out to tell Mum, Lizzie and the little kids and they run over.

Meg smiles and turns her head away so they won't see her pride and tease her.

Everyone gathers round Mavis and Meg, watching them dig, so nobody notices the thick black cloud roar up and spread out across the land. They're so engrossed in the digging they ignore the rush of wind and the first drops of rain that hit their backs.

They hear the parched soil hiss as it sucks the drops of moisture in, leaving dark wet circles in the grey earth. But still they keep digging. They dig and dig until the rain falls hard, stinging their backs, and lightning crackles across the sky. The cracks in the soil are full of water and raindrops are skidding across puddles like balls of silver before Mum yells, 'Come on. We're going to get struck by lightning,' and starts to run.

Mavis gets Alfred from Lizzie and runs with Mum, their clothes and hair stuck to their skin, the raindrops stinging their faces as they slip slide across the floodplain to the trees. Little Susan jiggles up and down on Mum's hip, laughing. The children yell, their arms outstretched to collect the rain. The women hold their skirts out from between their legs as they run. Meg gives up and follows. Caroleena and Lizzie stay digging. Digging with the crowbar and their fingers, scratching down till they get the crowbar under the shell and lift the turtle up out of the ground. Then, holding it tight around the neck, they run, following the squeals of laughter across the floodplain, up along the creek, through the dripping rainforest to the waterfall and back up to the camp.

5
Lost

Dale and Tomias run along the escarpment above Barrumbi, skipping and jumping over spinifex clumps, bouncing from rock to rock. The big rainstorm has moved on, crackling into the distance. The air is clean, leaves are bright green – the world's so bright it looks yellow.

'Yahhh! It worked! It worked, Tomias! They made it rain!' Dale yells. He's full of joy and wonder.

Tomias laughs and does a cartwheel over a big flat rock. They run along the escarpment to Barrumbi and look down over the waterfall to the pool where they played yesterday. There's no one there. It's too cold for swimming after the storm. Everyone must be back at the camp. They run past the spring and skip down the hill, kicking rocks to bounce chattering along beside them. Dale does a big downhill jump and his hat blows off. 'Bloody hell!' He has to skid to a stop, sliding onto his bum, and crawl back up the slope to get it. He can't leave it. His mum's totally paranoid about skin cancer and goes off her face if he doesn't wear his hat all the time. He stuffs it in his jeans pocket and runs down to catch up with Tomias.

The rock pool is still, dark and cool.

Tomias is walking along the edge of the pool, watching the still water. Dale sneaks up behind him, grabs him and gammon pushes him in. 'Hey!' Tomias yells, waving his arms about to keep his balance. He spins around to get Dale, but Dale slips past and runs up the little path through the rainforest to the camp.

Everyone's packing up.

There's a big wire cage around the back of the truck so everyone can sit in there without falling out. Dad's rolling down tarps over the sides to stop the rain coming in. Everyone else is packing, grabbing wet bags of clothes, swags, blankets, fishing gear and throwing them into the back, laughing and teasing each other, happy for the rain.

'Shake that blanket, good girl.'

'*Don't put that muddy one inside! Leave it!*'

'Mavis! That little Gloria not helping.'

Mavis looks at Gloria. She is living with Mavis at the moment because she is too naughty for her mother. 'Little Gloria?' Mavis says, teasing her. 'She nomore subbie. Djohboi! Poor thing.'

'I can so do it!'

'Nothing, you too small!'

'Look out! I gonna throw this one. Mightbe hit you na head!' Gloria yells, but she starts helping.

Mavis smiles.

The sun's out. It's warm, with a light breeze. The women and older girls wrap towels around themselves for modesty, to cover the wet dresses clinging to their legs.

'Better get going,' Dad says. 'There was a couple of inches in that storm – those blacksoil plains'll be slippery as buggery. And there's more to come.' He points up to the clouds still hanging over the escarpment.

Sandy nods and opens the bonnet to check the oil and water. Sandy's the best bush mechanic in the Territory, Dad reckons. 'Give him a piece of tie wire and he'll keep anything going.' He did his apprenticeship under Dad, even though he's an old man with white hair. He's Dad's best friend and Dale mob call him uncle.

While Mum and Dad stand talking to Sandy, Dale and Tomias run up to them. Dale grabs his hat out of his pocket and slams it on his head.

'Where's Sean?' Mum asks.

Dale and Tomias look at each other. 'Dunno.'

'Didn't you see him?' Dad says. 'I thought he'd be up there on the escarpment looking for snakes. We've got to go in a minute. He'd better hurry.'

Dale looks at Tomias.

Tomias puts his head down. He doesn't want to be involved if there's going to be big trouble.

Dad walks around the back of the truck. As soon as he's gone Dale whispers to Mum, 'We saw Sean up the back there before the storm.' He points over towards Death Adder Ridge.

'What? Where?' Mum's face is instantly white. Her green eyes flash.

Sandy looks up.

'Want us to go and sing out to him?' Dale asks.

She laughs. 'Dale, don't go making excuses to try and get out of packing up. You're not going back up there.'

'Mum, we did see him. Hey Tomias!'

She looks over at Tomias. Staring, waiting for him to look up. Waiting. Waiting.

Tomias tries to keep his head down but he can feel

her question burning into his head. He looks at her quickly, and when he does, she sees that Dale's telling the truth.

'Where was he – exactly?'

'Over that way. We were up here and he was over on that next hill – that way.'

Mum puts her hands over her face. 'Go on, run up there and sing out,' she says. Her stomach's churning. Little Susan on her hip feels the tension and starts to cry. Mum rocks her, holding her close, and looks up at Sandy, asking what she should do.

He looks back under the bonnet.

'Sandy?'

Sandy pulls his head out and climbs up onto the bull-bar, looking out into the sky. 'Lot of water that way.'

'That's Death Adder Ridge way,' she says in a whisper.

He ignores her – women shouldn't say that name. Even if they say it quiet, they shouldn't say it!

'Sandy?'

He keeps his head down.

'Sandy. He calls you uncle!'

'Old men there,' he says without looking up.

'Where?'

'That place now.'

'Will they watch for him?'

Sandy moves his head half way between a nod and a shrug and goes back under the bonnet.

Mum runs to tell Dad.

'Little smart-arse! What the bloody hell does he think he's doing? Serves him right if he does get stuck out there!' Dad says.

'You know what he's like at the moment. What if he's gone to Death Adder …'

'*I know!*' Dad yells. Then, softly, 'I know,' putting his arm around Mum. His lips are tight and he holds her close, looking over her shoulder at the black, black sky.

'We can't just leave him here.'

Silence.

It starts to rain again.

'Lucy, if we don't go now everyone will be walking home! Old Caroleena, all the little kids.'

'I've sent Dale and Tomias up there to sing out to him. We've got to wait at least until they get back.'

Mum's hair is wet and there's so much water running down her face it looks as if she's crying.

They pack. Everyone's quiet, whispering, 'Young boy – That place – Mightbe he bin die that one – Finish – Properly finish.'

Mavis goes over to stand with Mum. She's her sister. No matter what has happened, she has to stick up for her – and for Sean. If this had happened last year, Mavis would have been confident, knowing that Sean was properly grown up and would never go near that place. But something changed for Sean this year in town. It's like he's lost respect. So her heart is swelling with worry.

Caroleena and the little kids climb into the back of the truck and sit quietly. Jimmy puts Sean's swag against the wire and lies on top of it. Dad and Sandy sit in the cabin with Susan and Leroy. Mum walks around in the rain, looking up at the hill, down to the path coming up from the waterfall, expecting any minute that Sean will run up the track or sing out cheeky from the hill. Come on, she tells herself, have some faith in him, he wouldn't go there. He'll be back in a minute. He can't be lost. He's got his maps, his compass. He's careful.

But Sean doesn't come back.

Dale and Tomias run up the escarpment, calling, 'Sean! Sean!' Their voices echo back – nothing.

'Reckon he's there?' Dale asks.

Tomias shrugs his shoulders.

'Mavis reckons that no one comes back from there. Remember, she told us.'

Silence.

They look out at the country. There's a storm cloud over Death Adder Ridge, not moving at all. There's no lightning, just heavy rain, pouring rain, a thick black wall of water falling from the sky in that one place.

'Better go,' Tomias says.

'Just wait a bit,' Dale says, but Tomias is already jogging away.

'Cooee!' Dale keeps shouting across the land as he walks back, trying to stop the cold empty feeling spreading through his body. I should have told him, he thinks. I should have told him about the dream. I shouldn't have cared if he thought I was stupid. If he knew about the dream he definitely wouldn't have gone. He knows dreams can tell you things. Even Dad reckons that.

They slide down the slope to the waterfall pool. It looks eerie now, dark grey, reflecting the black cliffs on either side. Yesterday, when they arrived at

Barrumbi, the waterfall made such a beautiful trickling sound that they ran down through the forest to find it. Now it's violent and angry, pouring in a heavy stream of liquid metal over the cliff; bouncing, exploding into thousands of tiny particles that float like mist over the pool and into the rainforest.

The track's muddy and slippery. The breeze tickles the trees so the raindrops fall freezing cold onto the boys' bare skin, making them shiver. Ducking under leaves and branches, they run through the wet darkness and up into the light. The camp is empty. Everyone's in the back of the truck except Mum.

She looks at them and can see by the way they're walking, by the way they're shy to face her, that they've found nothing. She doesn't want to hear them say it, so she turns away, looking up at the ridge. Dale and Tomias go straight to the truck.

Dad goes over to Mum. 'Lucy? Another storm coming. If the truck goes down in that bog we'll have to leave it here all wet and walk home.'

'I know!' she says angrily. 'Something's wrong. I know it is.'

'Come on.' He puts his arm around her. 'We'll get everyone out and Sandy and I will come back in the Toyoda and get him.'

Mum walks to the truck without looking at anyone.

'S'all right Mum,' Leroy says, patting her leg. 'Don't be sad. Me and Lizzie aren't lost.'

Everything's wet in the back of the truck: the people, their clothes, the bedding. The air's heavy. Tarps flap, cracking in the breeze. Cold wind slips in, lifting goosebumps on their skin. Tomias and Dale sit on a wet swag, holding a hessian bag with two turtles in it to stop them bouncing against the wire. Everyone's shivering and quiet. The little kids curl up together, trying to get warm. Meg, Lizzie and Jeweleen have the only dry blanket, the one Mum put in the truck cab. They wrap it around themselves, snuggling up close. Jimmy lies back against Sean's swag and plays with his little radio, turning the dials, trying to find a station. A soft static crackles through the air.

The place behind the driver's seat, where Sean sat with the old men on the trip up to Barrumbi, is empty. It's the driest and most sheltered spot, but no one wants to sit there.

Caroleena keeps looking at the empty space and shakes her head. 'Poor thing. Poor thing.'

Dale wants to say, 'Sean hasn't gone there! He's not dead! What do you say "Poor thing" for?' But he doesn't.

'He better not go there. They'll kill him, finish,' says Reuben, Tomias's cousin. His almond eyes are narrowed, looking at Dale real smart.

Dale sneers at him. Reuben's so annoying, always trying to gammon that he knows all the laws and bush-tucker stuff. He's only the same age as Lizzie. What would he know?

Dale looks at Tomias, hoping Tomias will tell Reuben off. But Tomias says nothing. Reuben's always just trying to show off – don't worry about him.

One of the little kids starts coughing and then crying because she can't catch her breath between the coughs.

Caroleena motions with a curve of her hand: Dale, give that child to me.

Dale picks the little girl up and she's passed from person to person to Caroleena, who wraps her up warm, close to her skin, 'Ssh-ssh,' humming and rocking till the child is quiet.

The truck lurches down the escarpment over flat rocks and boulders, bouncing from side to side, skidding, the tyres slipping. Dad's swearing over the roaring motor as he tries to turn the truck into the slide and stop it from tipping over. The brakes burn, screeching metal on metal, and down the last steep rock everyone holds tight, tensing up as if to make themselves lighter.

The floodplain stretches out in front of them, glistening, black with moisture. Two tyre tracks cut it in half. Into second gear, engine roaring to build up speed, they start across, the truck slipping from side to side. Black mud sprays up from the wheels, spitting dark splats over Tomias and Dale who are sitting against the wire. Dale spins around, pulling down the tarp to cover the hole. He quickly ties it tight and sits back down.

'Look Dale's face!' The little kids laugh at his face, covered with spots of dark mud.

'What?' he says angrily, wiping with his hand, spreading the mud. They laugh louder. 'Shuddup,' Dale yells, and gammon tries to hit them. His face is dark and sour. He wants to hit them really hard. He wants to get up and go sit in the space behind the driver's seat – in Sean's space. Just sit there and look at everyone right in the eye. To wipe that frightened look from Mavis and Caroleena's faces, to show them Sean didn't do anything wrong. Make those little kids respect him, show them he's not frightened! He looks sideways at Tomias. Even him. He would even like to show Tomias.

Tomias sits as still as possible, trying to be invisible. His mind is racing, light with fear; his body heavy with dread. Just shut up, Dale, he thinks. He closes his eyes and tries to send mind messages to Dale. *Shut up. Make yourself small and humble.*

Mavis sees Dale's face twisted with anger. 'Look!' she says, pointing up at a large flock of magpie geese going across the sky in a V, their honking muffled by the roar of the engine. When the green grass sprouts all across the floodplain the geese will come in their thousands to feed. 'You got that gun Dale? You get that goose for me?' Mavis asks.

'Two. You get two for us,' Caroleena says. 'You and Tomias get plenty goose for us.'

Dale can't help himself; he has to smile, holding his lips tight and turning his head away. The boiling anger in his mind dissolves and he's filled with pride that Mavis and Caroleena think he can go hunting for them, that he's old enough to feed people.

Then the truck slips right off the road. Dad spins the wheel, jerking it this way and that, bumping over and back into the wheel ruts. Tomias and Dale hang onto the wire cage, holding themselves in place. Mavis and Caroleena are covered with little kids.

'Look out you mob!'

'Get your foot.'

'Come here, good girl.' The little girl's crying again because she got squashed. Caroleena picks her up and cuddles her. Looking out through the tarp at the escarpment, she sees the heavy blackness of cloud. The air's charged with electricity. We must get away from this place quickly, she thinks, holding tight to the child on her lap.

The truck climbs out of the floodplain onto the road. Behind it a huge darkness rolls over the escarpment. Lightning cuts the clouds in two. Wind whips leaves off trees, breaks branches and smashes them down on the rocks. And all the time rain pours from the sky, filling rock pools and dips, rushing into cracks and over ledges, tumbling from waterfalls down the escarpment, filling dry creeks and rivers and spreading out across the land.

6

Left Behind

The truck's slowing down. It stops.

Why? Can't see.

Must be at Chinaman Creek.

Dale puts his hand through the wire and unlocks the gate of the truck. Sunlight, sunshine. Everyone jumps out to stand in the warmth. Sandy and Dad walk down to the creek, Dale and Tomias right behind them. The water's roaring past, quick and dangerous. 'How come it's up so fast?' Dale asks. 'Hasn't even rained here.'

'From Barrumbi,' Tomias says.

'Already?'

Dad wades in a little way and stops – the current's strong, pulling at him.

Is it all right? Sandy asks, lifting his eyebrows.

'We'll get through!' Dad says. 'Get back in the truck, you kids.'

Sandy opens the bonnet, takes off the fan belt so it won't splash water all over the motor, and sprays the inside of the distributor with CRC.

Dad ties a big tarp over the bull-bar to push the water away from the motor. 'Come on, get in,' he says.

Dale's worried. What if the truck tips? What if it gets washed over the causeway into the creek? Everyone will be trapped in the back. All right for them in the front, he thinks. They can get out through the windows. But we'll be trapped.

'I'm not closing this door,' he says to Tomias. 'Leave it open so we can get out if we get washed off.' He sits near the door, holding it closed. 'Get back you kids or you'll fall out,' he says.

The tarp on the bull-bar pushes through the creek. It makes a huge wake on either side of the truck, keeping the water from pouring into the cage. Then one wheel falls down into a hole and the truck stops, the engine screaming. Before it can get going again, the wake drops and water rushes in the back through the wire cage, washing over everyone. The door swings open, dragging Dale out through the doorway.

'Look out!' Mavis yells, grabbing the little children as they start sliding with the water.

Dale's in the creek, his fingers clutching the wire door, his body dragging in the water.

'Dale!' Mavis screams. She grabs little Alfred, lifts him up.

Meg and Jeweleen are holding each other, shouting, 'Dale! Dale, hang on!' The truck lurches out of the hole and *swoosh*, all the water runs out again.

Tomias crawls over, grabs the door and pulls at it, but Dale's body dragging in the water makes it too heavy to close.

The rainwater that tasted Sean up in the gorge is now drifting in Chinaman Creek. It wraps itself around Dale's hot body, warming itself. Come, come, it says, come. It slips in under his shirt, stroking his chest, his arms. Come on, just let go, it says to his muscles. Come with me.

Dale can see everyone looking at him through the wire. They're all inside, he's outside. Serves them right if I do drown, he thinks. Serves them right for laughing at me. For getting angry at Sean, when they don't even know if he's done anything wrong. They don't care. They only care about the old men and spirits. They probably wish Sean was dead.

His arms are tired from hanging on. The water soothes him. He wants to let go and float down the creek.

Tomias stands reaching for Dale through the doorway.

'Careful, Tomias!' Meg screams.

'I got him,' Lizzie says. Standing behind Tomias, she holds onto his shirt and leans back. 'Grab onto me, Reuben.'

Tomias holds onto the door for leverage and reaches out for Dale. 'Give us ya hand.'

Piss off! Dale wants to say. Leave me! He stares at Tomias.

'Come on, get up!' Tomias yells at him.

The truck hits a bump and the door swings out farther.

Tomias falls forward, stretched between the door and Lizzie. Lizzie's legs are spread across the doorway, her arms wrapped around his legs.

'Tomias! Tomias, don't. You'll drown,' Dale yells. 'Leave me. I can get up.' Suddenly he has the strength to pull himself out of the water, up to the wire door.

The truck hits another bump. The door swings in.

Tomias is pushed back and Reuben drags him and Lizzie inside.

And Dale pulls his legs up out of the water. He clings to the wire door and Lizzie and Reuben drag it closed.

Dale's back inside the truck, breathing heavily, his arm leaning on Tomias's leg. He looks up at Reuben to say thanks. Reuben nods.

'Get away from that door!' Mavis yells at them, her voice angry. They move over against the wire. Meg covers Dale and Tomias with her wet blanket. Everyone's quiet.

'Don't tell Mum,' Dale says.

'No!' Meg and Lizzie say together. 'She'd have a heart attack.'

Tomias rests his head on his knees, remembering how Dale looked. He wanted to let go – you could see it. What's wrong with him?

Little kids cry softly, sniffling. Caroleena and Mavis grab them, laughing with relief that Dale isn't drowned and enjoying the little faces covered with tears and snot.

The truck climbs out on the opposite bank and stops. Everyone jumps out into the sunlight.

'What you mob doing?' Mavis and Caroleena yell at Dad and Sandy. 'We got water inside.' They pull their T-shirts off and wring the water out.

Meg and Jeweleen hold their blanket between them, twisting and twisting it into a rope. The water runs out, making a little river down the road.

Dale's legs are shaking. He leans against the tailgate.

That was spooky, he thinks. Like ... like something was there. Like when someone's watching you and you know it without seeing them ... Nah! Don't be silly. It's only the current, and because of Sean going lost. Don't think about it.

Mum doesn't get out of the truck. Little Susan calls, 'Lizzie, Lizzie' through the side window. Lizzie goes to pull her out of the cab, but seeing Mum's face so still and dark, she climbs up beside her instead. 'He'll be all right,' she says, putting her hand on Mum's shoulder.

'I know, love,' Mum says, her voice empty.

'I'll take Susan out in the sun.'

'No. Leave her here. Go and watch Leroy.' Mum looks back out the windscreen again.

'Jimmy's got him.'

'Well, help Jimmy,' Mum snaps, holding Susan tight to stop her climbing out.

By the time they get back to Long Hole it's dark. It's not raining yet but the smell is clear in the air. Dad stops to drop Mavis, Caroleena and Reuben mob at their homes. Tomias starts to get out with Mavis but Dale grabs his arm to tell him: Stay at my place.

'Can I stay with Lizzie?' little Gloria asks.

Mavis looks up at Mum to ask but Mum doesn't notice.

Little Gloria is real smart, she sees everything, so Mavis tells her, 'You stay with them,' nodding at Mum, telling Gloria to watch everything that happens at Dale's house and tell Mavis all about it.

Tomias is silent.

'We'll head straight back in the Toyoda so we get there at first light, before the river gets too high,' Dad tells Mum.

They're going back! Dale touches Tomias on the arm and looks at him to say, *Let's go!*

Tomias stares back at him in disbelief. Why? Why go back? There's something wrong out there. You don't mess around with stuff like that. But Dale doesn't notice.

Back at home, Mum and the kids get out. Mum goes to put Susan and Leroy to bed. 'Come on you boys,' she says to Dale and Tomias.

'We better help Dad,' Dale says.

'Nah. Me and Sandy'll be right,' Dad says.

'We could unload the truck while Dad and Sandy pack the Toyoda,' Dale says, holding his face real serious and open. He's talking to Mum. He knows that if he can convince Mum, she will get Dad to agree.

Mum thinks that with all the worry about Sean Dale's trying to be good, so she looks at Dad to say, Let him help. Please.

Dad looks away.

They go to the workshop. 'Get all the swags, spread them out to dry,' Dad says with a scowl.

Dale and Tomias work quickly, pulling all the swags out, unwrapping them and draping them over racks and lines to dry. 'There's a couple of dry ones, Dad. Will we put them in the Toyoda?' Dale asks.

'Yeah, chuck them in the back.'

Dale can hardly keep the smile off his face. He climbs up into the back of the Toyoda and places the swags so there's room for a couple of bodies to hide underneath them.

I'm not going, no matter what Dale says, Tomias thinks. As soon as we get back to Dale's place, I'm telling him I'm not going.

When all the stuff's packed they drive home through the black night, the car lights yellow in the wet air. 'Go on, off to bed you two,' Dad says.

'Come on.' Dale grabs Tomias and runs into the house. He hears Jimmy's radio in the bedroom. Can't go in there or he'll ask questions. He ducks into the bathroom. 'Put these on,' he says, handing Tomias some dirty but dry clothes.

Tomias is trying to get his words right. *I'm not going!* he wants to say. But Dale will think he's a sook. That he's scared of the dark. Dale will say, *What about Sean? Don't you care what happens to him?* And what can you say to that?

The light from the kitchen shines down the hallway, bringing murmuring conversations down to the waiting boys. Dale sneaks up the hall to hear what Mum and Dad are saying.

Dad and Sandy are drinking tea. Mum's walking up and down.

'Don't worry. He'll be there,' Dad says. 'The old blokes will look after him.'

'How will they know he's there? What if he's ...?' Mum can't say the words 'gone to Death Adder'; her voice is light and crackling.

Sandy turns his head away.

'Lucy, don't be ridiculous,' Dad says.

She starts to cry.

Dad puts his arm around her. 'Let's go,' he tells Sandy.

Come on. Dale waves to Tomias and slips out through the door. Tomias hesitates, but he has to follow. Dad and Sandy will see him if he stays standing in the hallway. Then Dale will get caught good and proper. So he follows Dale out into the dark and jumps up into the back of the Toyoda, ducking under the swags.

Dad comes out the door, his arm around Mum. 'It'll be right. Don't worry.'

Mum stands in the doorway, a silhouette.

'We'll be home with him in a couple of days,' Dad says, and his boots crunch towards the Toyoda.

'Please don't let them see us,' Dale whispers under his breath. 'Please don't let them get anything out of the back and catch us! Please! Please! Please!'

The car doors slam. The engine starts up and they drive off down the road.

The boys keep their heads down under the swags for ages. Dale's smiling so much his cheeks hurt. He can't believe they got away with it. We're the best! he thinks. The absolute best!

That's it, Tomias thinks. You're dead meat, Dale. His eyes narrow with anger. As soon as he gets the chance he's going to hit Dale hard, really hard. Dale's always making people do things they don't want to.

They drive for miles and miles before Dale's game enough to sit up and whisper, 'Tomias.'

Tomias is still angry. So, when he sees Dale's smiling face, and his arm out to slap hands together to say, We did it!, he grabs Dale's hand and arm-wrestles him. Both of them strain across a swag till Tomias wins. Then he holds Dale's hand down and squeezes it till his fingers hurt, looking hard into his eyes. Dale smiles. 'We did it!' he whispers, and laughs.

Tomias laughs too. He has to. Dale's such a dickhead.

There's blackness all around them. They find a comfortable place, lying down with their heads resting on the swags, and watch the black starless sky. They fall asleep, bumping along in the dark.

Just as the morning light's turning the sky grey, they wake up.

Shit! It's starting to get light. How're we gonna stay hidden? They peek at Dad and Sandy in the front, driving along in silence, their faces serious in the rear-view mirror.

7
Signs of Life

The Toyoda stops. It's about six o'clock in the morning.

The boys slip down under the swags again to hide.

Car doors open.

Crunch. Crunch. Dad and Sandy walk down to Chinaman Creek.

Dale and Tomias peek through the back window to watch. The creek's twice as high; it's like a river. They'll never get through now, not even with the Toyoda. Dad pokes a stick into the soil at the waterline.

The men sit on their haunches, watching; they roll and light cigarettes. The water's rising, rising quickly, coming up and covering the stick before they finish their smoke.

'They're coming,' Dale whispers, and he and Tomias duck down.

In silence Dad and Sandy walk back, get in the Toyoda, reverse it to the top of the hill where it won't get washed away if the creek comes right up. They grab their guns from behind the seat. Dad reaches into the back to get his backpack; his hand comes so close that Tomias smells the cigarette smoke on his fingers. The men's footsteps crunch away, down towards the river.

The boys are too scared to get out in case they come back, so they stay peeking through the window, watching them turn off the road, cutting through the bush, heading upstream. The river's raging. How the hell are they going to get across? Then Dad and Sandy are in the water, holding their rifles above their heads, swimming sideways. The current pulls them quickly downstream. They're going past! Dad grabs a branch, throws his gun up on the bank and stretches his arm out to Sandy. They disappear among the trees downstream.

Minutes later they come squelching out of the bush on the other side. They lean their rifles against a tree, take off their clothes, wring them out – their bums, one black, one white, standing together.

No shame.

Dale looks away and then back. He's never seen his dad naked before. He looks really skinny and white, small and soft.

Dad and Sandy get dressed, and with their guns over their shoulders they climb up the bank and walk down the long red road.

Standing up on the roof of the Toyoda, Dale watches them till their bodies are just fuzzy dark lines. They go into a dip and disappear. He jumps down and runs up the hill on the side of the road, trying to keep them in sight.

'Whatcha doing?' Tomias yells after him.

Dale doesn't answer. He doesn't know what he's doing. It's just that he's scared for his dad. He wants to keep looking at him. He climbs higher and higher, looking over his shoulder. The ground's made of broken red rocks, shale. He has to move quickly, stumbling, tripping. He falls, scrapes his knee; it's bleeding. He loses sight of Dad and Sandy. Then he sees them again, little black dots in the huge landscape. On either side the flat-top hills are purple, their sheer cliffs at the top like collars of light. The land falls away from them into deep valleys. From this height Dale can see far beyond the river to the floodplains, shining silver and blue, reflecting the sky. They're full of water. Beyond them the escarpment rises up from the flatness like an enormous castle, its turrets, towers and battlements making weird shapes on the horizon. He climbs up on a large rock to watch the two black dots wading into a floodplain. What about crocodiles? he thinks.

The rocks around Dale are bright red, wet with the rain. There's no spear grass – it was burnt months ago in the early Dry season. The spear grass seeds that screwed themselves into the soil are now coming to life, swelling, turning yellow, the green shoots inside them itching to burst out into the sun. In a few days they will emerge, covering the ground like a mass of fine bright green spikes. Gnarled gums cling to the rocks, their skin folding in creases as the branches twist and turn – orange bark lifting to expose new pink skin. Turkey bush flowers, recently fallen, litter the ground: tiny brown star-shapes, their bright pink colour gone. Dead turkey bush branches twist out of the soil or lie broken over the red rocks like driftwood.

'*Dale! Dale!*' Tomias yells, his voice loud and shrill.

Dale jumps up. Tomias is down by Chinaman Creek. Probably saw a croc. No – he's wading into the water. What's he doing? He's got something, carrying something. Running flat out up towards the Toyoda.

'Dale!'

'What? What?'

'Sean's boot!'

'Sean's boot. What you mean, Sean's boot? No way!'

Tomias holds up a dark wet boot. 'Sean's boot!' He's panting.

'Shit. If it's Sean's ...' Dale runs over. Can't be! Please don't make it ... But before he touches its blackness, he can see Sean's laces made of rawhide. Kangaroo skin, de-haired, cut into thin, thin strips, tied to a tree and stretched with a big rock to weigh them down, twisted each day while they cured.

Tomias holds the boot out. 'Here,' he says. He doesn't want to hold it but can't let it drop. Dale won't take it. They both stare. The boot drips, drips. Dead! Sean must be dead, drowned.

Aloud, Dale says, 'Your boots don't come off if you drown.' Then, just to prove him wrong, Sean's dead body flashes into his mind, white, bloated, disintegrating, being eaten, torn to pieces by yabbies and fish, ripped apart by crocs and turtles, the boot floating away empty, pieces of Sean following.

'What if he's ...'

They run back to the river, Tomias still holding the boot.

'Where?'

'It was stuck!' Tomias says, pointing to a big tree with water swirling round it. 'Look like a possum.' He shudders, remembering how he saw the boot, the dead person's boot, rocking gently against the trunk. He touched a dead person's boot! But at that moment he didn't think. When he saw it he knew Sean was dead. But he had to show Dale. He didn't think about if he got sick or what. He didn't stop himself. Now he realises he's still holding it. He quickly puts the boot on the ground and steps back.

They sit and watch the river in silence, the boot between them. The water rushes past, its movement drawing them in. Do pieces of human float? Whole bodies do float, Dale's sure of that. In the pictures and on the radio they're always finding bodies floating.

There's something! A dark patch. Sean?

A twig full of leaves.

Nothing. Nothing. For ages there's nothing.

There's something hairy in the water! – Sean's head?

No, a dead possum.

Both their hearts are nearly bursting, pumping so hard their arms are tingling. Don't look. A body floats better than a boot. If he was dead, he would have floated past ages ago.

Dale turns and looks at the boot, his mind arguing with itself.

The laces are undone! He must have taken it off. He's not dead!

But if he went for a swim he would take his boots off. He might have gone swimming and drowned.

Nah. Sean wouldn't go near the water once the rain started. He knows about flash flooding, where the water comes down like a wall, killing everything in its road. He wouldn't!

But you thought Sean wouldn't go to Death Adder Ridge!

He might not have! No one knows what's happened!

There's a shrill cry in the sky. A hawk circles high above them.

That's weird. In the Dry season there are hundreds of shit hawks hanging around, following the fires, floating up on the rising heat, scanning the burnt earth for fleeing animals. But what's this one doing here? You don't see them much this time of year. Not hanging around circling. Maybe a road kill? Nah. We didn't hit anything and no one's come past since. It must be hunting. Snake? Goanna? Maybe it's going to grab something out of the flooding water.

Both boys stay absolutely still so they don't frighten the bird. Their eye muscles hurt trying to look up at the hawk and down to check for animals without moving their heads.

Lower and lower the hawk circles. It's got something, a snake or something in its feet. Why doesn't it just go and eat it? Why fly around with food? With each circle the hawk comes closer and closer.

That's not a snake! It's like a rope or something dangling from its leg!

'Hey! Mightbe Sir Galahad. You know, Sean's hawk. He took off with that whatsitcall on his leg,' Dale whispers. 'Can you make that whistle? Like Sean?'

Tomias slowly lifts his hand up to his lips, and with his fingers between his teeth, pushing his tongue back, he whistles two short bursts.

The hawk quickly turns, scanning the ground with interest.

'That's it! Look, him subbie. That's him now!' Dale says. 'Go on!'

Tomias whistles again. 'Put your arm.'

Very slowly Dale stands up, walks a little way from Tomias and stretches his arm out like Sean used to do. Tomias whistles again and again, and the hawk comes closer till they can see the jess clearly. Then he hovers for a moment and comes swooping down towards Dale. Dale closes his eyes to stop himself pulling his hand away at the last minute. He concentrates with all his might on keeping his arm out stiff.

Swoosh, Sir Galahad goes right past, so close the wind from his wings rushes at Dale's face. He lands in a tree farther up the hill.

Tomias whistles softly, and both boys walk over the rocks to get closer. Sir Galahad cocks his head from side to side, his yellow eyes untrusting.

'It's okay, Sir Galahad,' Dale says.

'Make out like you got food,' Tomias whispers.

'Come on mate.' Dale's stretched out one of his arms; he holds the other up, his fingers curled into a loose fist. 'Come on. Get food.'

Sir Galahad spreads his wings, jumps into the air and swoops down. He lifts his feet and lands on Dale's arm.

His long talons dig deep into flesh. Dale's eyes open wide, his mouth goes *Owww!* He keeps his arm still, but it's starting to shake with the pain. *That's why they wear gloves!*

Tomias sniggers, his eyes crinkling, his mouth tight. 'Grab that rope.'

Dale can't take his eyes off the hawk's talons. If he scares the bird, it'll rip his arm to pieces.

'Grab that rope,' Tomias says again.

Dale reaches up and takes hold of the jess. Sir Galahad leans down to take food from Dale's hand and finds none. He digs his talons in deeper, jerking his head forward.

Dale closes his eyes.

'Look at that leg!' Tomias says, moving closer.

One leg's all lumpy.

'Gotta take that rope off, his leg's buggered.'

Dale holds the jess tight. 'Don't scare him.'

Sir Galahad feels the tension on the jess and panics, spreading his wings, trying to take off. His huge wings slap against Dale's face. Dale's other hand rushes to grab the bird, collides with wings and feathers. The hawk's flapping, frantic and screaming, its high-pitched cry filling the air.

Tomias whips off his T-shirt and throws it over Sir Galahad, pushing him down on the ground. Finally, in the darkness under the shirt, with four hands holding him, Sir Galahad is still.

Blood drips down Dale's arms.

Tomias wraps the hawk up tight so he can't move and opens the shirt to see the jess.

'Look,' Dale says, pointing. One leg is badly deformed, the skin swollen at either end of a pale patch.

He lifts the other leg, the one with the jess on. 'This one's okay.'

'It was on this foot,' Tomias says, running his fingers over the leg where it's raw and dented; where the jess was on too long. 'Look.' He lifts the jess up to show Dale. The skin underneath it is normal. It's not even pale. The jess has only just been put on. Hasn't been there for more than a day.

Tomias and Dale look at each other.

'Sean! It's gotta be Sean!' Dale says, his voice loud with excitement. 'Sir Galahad couldn't've got the jess off himself. And he wouldn't put it back on. It's gotta be Sean. He must've caught him and changed it.'

Tomias unties the jess and holds it up. Dale puts the bird down carefully, undoing the T-shirt. Sir Galahad stands, blinking for a minute, turning his head right around to look at them. The boys stay still. Sir Galahad skips up onto a small rock; stops with a shocked look on his face; bends his head down to check out his feet. He jumps to a larger rock. There's nothing flapping beneath him! He jumps again, lifting his feet one by one to test their weight, and then he launches himself into the air, his wings flapping lazily. They watch him rise higher and higher, flying away towards the escarpment. Wonder if he's going back to Sean?

Tomias is still holding the jess.

Dale reaches for it. 'What d'ya reckon? Must've been Sean. It was changed, hey. Has to be Sean!'

Just then the Toyoda motor starts.

8

In Trouble Again

'*Dad!* Run! They're leaving!' Dale takes off for the Toyoda. 'Dad! Wait!'

The car's across the road, reversing, doing a three-point turn. 'Dad! Sean's ...' Dale runs onto the road in front of the Toyoda, arms up.

'*What the hell!*' Dad slams on the brakes.

Dale sees Dad's face and he realises that he's in big trouble. Big, big trouble. 'Oh-ow.' He looks around at the bush in panic.

Dad pulls on the handbrake and jumps out of the car. '*What the bloody hell are you –*'

Dale knows there's no use trying to explain. He turns around and races down to the creek.

'*Get back here, you little bastard!*' Dad yells.

Tomias is standing by the side of the road, absolutely still.

Dale grabs the boot and runs back up the hill. 'Found Sean's boot, Dad. Was in the river. He took it off. He's not dead. We caught Sir Galahad. He had his jess changed.'

'What?'

'Sean's boot.' Dale hands it to Dad. 'We found it in the river. The laces were already undone. We caught Sir Galahad, remember, Sean's hawk? He still had his jess on. It was on the other leg.' Dale's voice is getting higher and higher and he's stepping back out of Dad's reach.

Dad's looking at the boot, holding it in both hands. His face all weird.

'Sean undone the laces and took his boots off,' Dale continues.

'What're you saying about the hawk?' Dad asks, his voice quiet.

'His jess. It was changed. His one leg was all busted from where the jess was too tight but it was on the other foot. Sean changed it to the other foot! It has to be Sean!' Dale's words tumble over one another, trying to make Dad understand.

'Where is it?'

'What?'

'The jess.' Dad's eyes are still narrow and cold. He's listened to hundreds of Dale's stories and doesn't know whether to believe this one or not.

Tomias walks over, and, leaning forward, keeping his body as far away from Dad as possible, he hands him the jess.

'One leg was all skinny, with sort of bumps where it was growing over the jess. Like, you know how trees grow a lump around fencing wire – like that. But the jess was on the other foot. The clean one,' Dale says, trying to speak more slowly so Dad can understand.

Dad takes the jess, stretches it out between his hands. *Sean made this. Perfect workmanship.* His eyes go cloudy and tears constrict his throat. He blinks a couple of times.

'And what do you think your mother's thinking,

Dale? You bloody selfish little bugger. She's lost one son already!'

'He's not lost. He's not dead. He can't be dead, Dad, the jess was ...'

Dad turns the jess over and looks at the other side. 'Shut up, Dale,' he says quietly, his tone changed, softer.

He holds the jess up to the light. There's something on it, letters scratched into it with a rock or something.

MUM IM SAFE – SEAN.

Dad's mouth opens, and there really are tears in his eyes. Dale can see his Adam's apple bounce up and down as he swallows.

'Get in the back!' he says, jerking his thumb over his shoulder. He takes the boot and the jess and climbs into the driver's seat of the Toyoda.

Tomias and Dale jump in quickly, thankful they didn't get a hiding. They lean against the window. There must've been a message on the jess. It was like Dad was reading something.

Dale turns round to look at Dad and Sandy through the window. Dad's talking, talking, talking; showing Sandy the jess, pointing at the boot on the seat between them. Sandy reaches out and takes the jess. Sandy believes that Sean's alive! He's holding the jess and reading the message! The message? Dale puts his head close to the glass and tries to see what it says but the glass distorts it. He can't see.

As soon as they get home, Dad jumps out of the car with Sean's boot and jess and goes in to tell Mum. Dale and Tomias stay in the back of the Toyoda. Neither of them wants to face Mum. When she gets mad she really goes off. Best to wait till Dad tells her the good news. She'll still go berko but at least she'll be a bit happy if she knows Sean's okay. They look at each other, remembering the last time they were in big trouble. That was the worst! They got grounded for a whole term. There's still weeks of holidays left. God, please don't let her think about grounding again.

Dad's gone for ages. So long that Dale starts thinking they should sneak away and camp at Tomias's place for the night. But before he has the chance to suggest anything, Dad comes out the door saying, 'Better get in and see your mother! You too, Tomias,' and hops back in the car with Sandy.

Sandy and Dad sit in silence for a moment. Then Dad says in language, 'We need to get the police. Get them to go and look for Sean. They can go up there with a helicopter.'

Sandy frowns.

'I know it's a sacred place but … Is there anyone here who can give us permission?' Dad says again in language.

Silence.

'I know it's asking a lot. He's just a kid. I'll make sure he gets punished!' Dad's fumbling, trying to find a word for a young man without knowledge who breaks the laws; a word that doesn't say he's a criminal. 'We can't just leave him out there.'

'Old men there,' Sandy says.

'But …'

Silence.

'Okay, forget about the police. What about if we go. Get a helicopter to take us up there and drop us off. Can you go in there?'

Sandy looks up for the first time to meet Dad's eyes.

'I can go there,' he says in English.

'Can we go in just to make sure he's with the old men? We don't have to bring him home – just make sure he's alive. For Lucy. His mother needs to know that he's alive or she will die inside,' he says in language, and then, to accentuate his meaning, he says it again in English: 'Properly sad.'

'Mum?' Dale says as he and Tomias walk through the door.

'You're back,' Mum answers without looking up.

'They couldn't get through the floodplain.'

'Yes, Dad said.'

Dale and Tomias don't know what to do. Mum isn't even looking at them. She's just sitting at the table with Sean's boot and the jess in her hands. They expected her to yell and scream at them, to carry on about how worried she was. But she's really calm. Not mad at all about them sneaking away.

They stand there, not moving. Jimmy waits in the other doorway, worried that Dale and Tomias will get in the biggest trouble. He looks at them, lifting his eyebrows to say: What's happening?

They shrug their shoulders: Don't know.

Finally Mum says, 'Have you got something to say?'

'Sorry. We're really sorry. We didn't mean to worry you but . . .' Dale walks towards her.

'Well, you can thank Mavis.'

'Mavis?' Tomias's eyes get larger. Mavis will be really mad if she finds out that he touched that boot.

'Yes, she came up and let me know where you were before I even missed you. Gloria saw you climb in the back of the Toyoda and told Mavis.'

They stand there waiting, waiting. Then Dale nods to Tomias that they should sneak away. They're just turning around when Mum says, 'Lucky you did go or we wouldn't have these.' Wrapping the jess around her wrist like a bracelet, she lifts it up and kisses it and holds it against her cheek. She's like a zombie, quiet and dead inside.

'They'll get him, Mum,' Dale says.

'I know, love.'

'He can find bushtucker. He won't do nothing stupid. The old men will look after him.'

Mum looks up at Dale and tries to smile. 'I know, love. I know.' She reaches out to Dale, but Tomias is watching so Dale moves away, embarrassed. Her hands fall into her lap.

Opium River, a nearby station, has a helicopter mustering cattle up into high ground for the Wet. They send it over straight away.

It lands in the schoolyard. The young pilot jumps from the belly and walks out, bent over, from under the rotating blades. The engine's still running.

'Is your young fella lost?' he asks Dad, yelling over the roar of the motor.

Dad nods.

'Don't worry, we'll find him. We can get right down into those gutters. This thing manoeuvres like a motorbike.'

'Can you drop us off at the ridge above Barrumbi? We'll walk in from there.'

'Barrumbi?' The pilot looks confused.

'Rock hole.' Dad points up into the escarpment.

'Ahh, Missionary Rock Hole.'

'Can you just drop us off ...?'

'Only one. I only have room for one passenger.'

Dad stands thinking for a moment. 'Could you hang on a minute?' He walks over and talks to Sandy and comes back. 'Sandy's going to go. He knows where the place is.'

'I know where the place is! I could drop you right into it.'

'Look, it's a bit touchy, this whole business. Can you just drop Sandy off where he asks and pick him up from the same place? I think he'll want to go to Missionary Rock Hole and he'll walk the rest of the way in.'

The young bloke shakes his head. 'Whatever!' he says, rolling his eyes. 'But if it was my kid ...'

Yes, Dad thinks, staring at the young man. If it was your kid it would be easy.

The pilot looks away, embarrassed, but Dad keeps staring at him. His mind rages. You'd just fly in, wouldn't you. You could bring in the army, have tanks smashing up this sacred place, running over everything. You don't know and you don't care. You're lucky. But I have to do the right thing.

The young man looks back at Dad's silence and meets his angry eyes. 'Sorry,' he says.

'No, it's all right.' Dad shakes his head. 'He's up there with some old men I trust,' he says, as much to convince himself as the young pilot. 'And Sandy, he knows the country. I know Sandy'll find him and bring him home. I know he'll be all right.'

The young man nods. Calling Sandy with a curve of his hand, he ducks under the twirling blades and climbs into the helicopter.

Dale and Tomias stand watching from the fence. The motor gets louder and louder, screaming in their ears. Dad doesn't move. Everyone else walks back away from the wind, but Dad just stays there. The chopper blades spin, spinning so fast they whip grass and leaves up from the damp ground, blowing his clothes and hair, lifting his hat and tossing it away across the schoolyard. He doesn't notice. He stands like a wooden pole stuck in the ground.

Lizzie runs to grab Dad's hat and walks over to him. She stands beside him and takes his hand, and together they watch the helicopter lift, tip forward, and take off over the school, into the grey sky.

The whole community stops to watch the helicopter until it's just a tiny speck in the distance.

9

The Wet Sets In

As soon as the helicopter leaves, it starts to rain and the kids race home. Sharp gusts of wind break small branches and they fall, *clunk*, on the tin roof. The wind sneaks in through the door, chilling exposed skin. It rains and rains and rains. The sound of it comes in waves; heavy and fast for a while and then gentle and slow, but always raining. The roads turn into puddles.

Mum and Dad sit at the kitchen table, talking, talking, waiting. The helicopter has just left, but already they're listening for it to come back, their ears alert, concentrating. Neither of them wants to admit that they're worried, not even to each other. They know the old men will look after Sean, but what if he isn't with them? What if he's been bitten by a death adder? They struggle against the urge to call the police, to get Sean out right now. Not to worry about respect and proper behaviour. But they wait, hearts swollen and aching.

The kids are worried about Sean too. Of course they are. But the rain's washing the country to a rich green, the breezes are light with moisture. The grey sky softens the edges, smooths all the sharp lines. Their eyes, so used to narrowing against the white-hot glare of the

Buildup, relax into this softness. They sit watching the rain through the louvres.

Dale wants to go outside and play, but he feels guilty, with Sean and all. He and Lizzie look at each other.

Sean's all right, Dale thinks. Of course he is! He didn't go to Death Adder Ridge and die. The jess and the boot prove that. He's with the old men. Sandy's gone to bring him home. I bet he's having a great time, camping up in the escarpment, playing in the rock pools, catching lizards and snakes. Mum's just going off. She always goes over the top.

Just then the wind blows and a fine mist slips through the louvres, covering their faces with coolness. Dale touches his cheek, and suddenly he's in prison and he has to get out. He catches Tomias's eye and points with his chin to say, Let's go outside. Lizzie's already made up her mind and is slipping out the door, Gloria and Reuben at her heels.

Dale and Tomias take off before Jimmy can follow them. So Jimmy follows Lizzie mob. The four younger children run through the warm rain, their clothes wet, clinging to their bodies. They wash themselves under broken gutter pipes. The gutters run, tanks overflow, puddles join to make little rivers in the drains on each side of the road.

Then the rain stops and the sun comes out, sucking the moisture up from the ground into the steamy air. And they make mud shoes. They walk in the fine silt clay of the open drain so it sticks to their feet, then they sit down and let it dry a bit, and then they walk in it some more until they have huge boots of mud. They stomp around, their feet heavy; they gammon kick each other and make weird tracks on the road.

'Hey, there's fish! There's fish in the drain!' Jimmy yells. And there are, millions of them swimming in the muddy water. The kids rush over to catch the little fish in cupped hands, tiny silver wiggles with big eyes.

'How come there's fish?' Jimmy asks.

'Up that spring?' Reuben says.

'Nothing! From that rain!' Lizzie argues.

Jimmy and Reuben laugh at her. But her face is serious.

'True!' she says. 'It's in that book. They come from that cloud. That fish egg get sucked up na cloud. When that rain come,' she says, and motions that the fish fall with the rainwater.

Jimmy screws up his face. 'Right!'

'You myall!' Lizzie says, losing patience. She walks down the drain to a deep spot and sits down, the water up to her neck. 'You subbie nothing.'

'Reckon it's true?' Jimmy asks as they follow her.

Reuben shrugs his shoulders.

'I reckon it's true!' Gloria says. 'That'd be cool. Swimming na cloud.'

Their skin's sticky with sweat so they all sit in the open drain, the muddy water heavy in their hands. The silt catches and dries in their hair, on their bodies, lining the creases in their clothes, coating their skin with a light film of dust, soft like powder. On Gloria's black skin it dries white, on Reuben's brown skin it goes yellow, and on Lizzie and Jimmy's white skin, it dries brown.

*

Meg and Jeweleen are on Meg's bed, listening to the rain drumming on the roof. They've made hot Milos and dressed up in flannel shirts and jeans – pretending it's winter time and they live down south in their own apartment. They comb each other's hair and try on Meg's new hair ties.

Jeweleen loves Meg's hair: it's the colour of dark red dirt, and curly. She makes lots of little plaits and ties them at the end with bright strips of cloth and pins them up on Meg's head with green butterfly clips.

Meg loves Jeweleen's hair: it's beautiful, black and silky. In a ponytail, it bounces when she walks along – so cool. Meg pulls Jeweleen's hair up high on her head and splits her ponytail into lots of little strings, catching each one with a different coloured butterfly clip. They make up the best hairstyles.

Later, they go outside to watch Dale and Tomias racing through the puddles on their bikes. The water caught in the spokes makes the wheels look solid, and the mud sprays up the boys' backs in a line, giving them a red mohawk from their pants to the top of their heads.

'Have a competition for best wheelie?' Jeweleen yells to them.

'Yeah!' Tomias says, and races down the road to get a good run-up. As he hits a big puddle he lifts his bike up and rides all the way through it with the front wheel spinning in the air like a silver disc.

Meg and Jeweleen clap and giggle. In their minds they are beautiful women at the motor races, cheering on the famous drivers.

‘My go!’ Dale takes off down the road to get ready.

Tomias grins at the girls and pulls a big log into the puddle. It disappears under the water.

‘Tomias?’ Meg says.

‘S’all right. Just a joke.’

Further up the road Dale’s just turning round, ready to do the big run-up and fly through the puddle. He doesn’t see Tomias make the trap.

Everyone’s watching – even Jeweleen. Dale wants to do a really cool wheel stand like Tomias. Got to go really fast so you can stay up for a long time! He rides standing up, throwing the bike from side to side as he pushes his feet down hard one after the other, speeding along, his eyes focused on the puddle. Nearly there now – lift …

Meg’s running towards the puddle. ‘Stop! Dale, stop!’

What she doing? *A dark line! Shit! There’s something in the puddle!*

Dale screeches on the brakes and spins the back wheel, skidding into the muddy water, sending it spraying into the air. All over Tomias! That’ll teach him!

‘Whatcha do that for! Could’ve killed me, Tomias!’ Dale yells as the bike stops.

Tomias is laughing, he’s bent over laughing, wiping the mud from his face, spitting it out of his mouth and laughing so much his belly hurts.

Dale smiles. It *is* a bit funny.

Jeweleen and Meg!

He sees Jeweleen and Meg standing there, hands by their sides, both of them covered with mud. Meg wipes her face, takes one step forward. ‘*Dale!*’ Her face is curled into a snarl, eyes like fire, hands raised to scratch him to death.

He lifts his bike up, spins it round, jumps on it and bolts.

'I'm telling Mum!' he hears Meg yell. *'Dale, you're dead meat!'*

Dale and Tomias fly down the road, going straight through the puddles, sending mud spinning up into the air.

Lizzie mob are playing in the drains by the creek.

'Let's play war,' Dale yells to them.

'Yeah!'

The first rains pick up leaves and bits of grass and drop them in the drains, making ripples of silt and debris. This is the best stuff for making bombs.

'Me and Tomias against you mob.'

'Not fair!' Jimmy says.

'Okay, you can come with us, Jimmy.'

Dale, Tomias and Jimmy sit in one drain, the rest of the kids in the other. They're fighting for control of the road.

'Right,' Dale whispers. 'We'll make the balls and Tomias can fire them.'

'Why?'

'He's a crack shot. We'll win!'

He sits down. 'Make your bombs like this,' he says to Jimmy, mixing wet mud, drier dirt with lots of little stones in it, and plenty of wet grass.

'Shouldn't put stones,' Jimmy says.

'That's shrapnel! All bombs gotta have shrapnel!'

Whacking the bomb from hand to hand, he tells him, 'Smash them like this to make them really hard.'

As soon as they've got a line of bombs Tomias starts firing.

The other mob retaliates, making everyone duck.

Dale jumps up. 'Cover me,' he says, and crawls out of his drain. 'We've got the road!' he yells to the other mob. Tomias and Jimmy are throwing a hail of bombs to protect him.

'No way! Dale's got the road!' Lizzie stands up to look and one of Tomias's bombs hits her, exploding on her bare shoulder and making a red mark. Her back stings, but she sneaks up again. Dale's in the middle of the road! Once he gets to this side his mob'll win! Gotta stop him, she thinks. 'Reuben, cover me!' she yells. She grabs a handful of bombs, jumps up out of the drain, and *smash, smash, smash*, she hits Dale on the head and the back. Tomias's bombs hit her arm and her belly but she doesn't care. 'Got ya! You're dead!' she yells at Dale, ducking back into the drain.

But Dale keeps coming.

Lizzie stands up and yells, 'You're dead!' Bombs whiz past her.

'Am not! Ya just blew me arm off!'

'Gammon, them bombs is full a shrapnel. Ya guts is cut open,' Reuben says. He jumps out of the drain and wrestles Dale to stop him coming any closer, and it starts to rain again, heavy warm rain. The drain's filling with water, so they all run down towards the creek to shelter under the paperbarks.

'You mob cheat! You got no shame,' Lizzie says.

'Hey, not me!' Tomias says.

'That's your side now,' Reuben says. 'You cheater too.'

'It's only gammon anyway. You can't have cheats with gammon,' Dale says, screwing his face up. 'You mob just jealous.'

'You were dead, Dale!'

Dead?

Everyone's silent under the paperbarks. Shouldn't say 'dead'. What if Sean did get bitten by a death adder? What if he is dead? Shouldn't joke about things like that.

10

Walking the Knife Edge

When Dale and Tomias come in for dinner, everyone's already sitting down at the table. The rain tinkles softly on the roof.

'Where the hell have you been?' Dad growls.

Dale's just opening his mouth, trying to find a good excuse, when the radio calls out, 'Opium River calling Long Hole. Opium River calling Long Hole.'

Mum jumps up and rushes to answer, 'Long Hole. Over,' her voice high with expectation and hope.

'Dropped the old fella off. Will pick him up day after tomorrow, over,' says the young pilot's voice.

'Oh, did you drop him at Barrumbi – Missionary Rock Hole escarpment? Over.'

'Yeah. Over.'

'Lucy?' A woman's voice is now on the phone. 'Lucy, are you okay? Oh, what a stupid question. Is there anything I can do?'

'No,' says Mum. 'We just have to wait.' And suddenly her shoulders are shaking. 'No, but thanks anyway.' It sounds like she's going to cry. 'Do you have a bigger chopper handy? They'll need to carry two people on the way back. Over.' Her voice is bright and crackly.

'Yep. We'll check it out. We're keeping our fingers crossed for him. Over.'

'Thanks, Bev. Over and out.'

Two days later they hear the chopper in the distance. Everyone in the community, the council workers, middle camp and top camp, all stop what they're doing and come running up to the school to see.

The helicopter hovers over the schoolyard while the adults chase the kids off the oval so it can land. Kids and dogs run in all directions; everyone laughs, excited that Sean's coming back.

Finally the oval's clear and the helicopter lands.

Mum, Leroy and Susan come running up from the house. It's a small chopper. It's not a four-seater. But Sean could be in the luggage rack behind the seats. *Please. Please make him be in there.*

Mum watches as the helicopter settles. The pilot doesn't get out. Dad ducks under the blades and runs in to talk to him. Sandy steps out the other side. Dad's yelling over the roaring motor, his arms moving to make his words clear.

Mum turns and starts walking away.

Leroy pulls back against Mum's hand. 'I wanta stay with Dad! I wanta stay with Dad!'

Mum's hand tightens on his and she walks quicker and quicker until Leroy's getting pulled along, taking really long steps to keep up. '*Daddy! Daddy!*' he yells, turning his head back towards the helicopter.

Dale and Tomias watch Leroy crying all the way down the road. The helicopter leaves and suddenly the day's empty and grey – silent. They wander around the oval, kicking cans, not talking.

Lizzie follows Dad, trying to help him. He nearly trips over her and yells, 'Get out from under my feet!' She walks off, angry tears in her eyes.

Mum sits at the kitchen table. Leroy and Susan run around doing whatever they like.

Sandy and Dad come home, Meg and Jeweleen right behind them. 'Take the kids down to the bedroom, Megan,' Dad says, his face serious.

'What happened? Where's Sean?' Meg asks.

'Quick!' he answers, pointing to the room.

They go. But Meg can't just sit down in the bedroom and wait. 'Keep these mob down here,' she whispers to Jeweleen, and she sneaks outside, slipping round the corner and hiding down in the bush beside the kitchen window to listen to Mum and Dad.

Mum's making tea. 'They reckon there's a lot more rain coming,' she says.

Dad and Sandy are sitting at the table. It's hard for Sandy to talk while Mum's listening – even if he calls her his sister. He doesn't want to say important names while a woman can hear.

Mum doesn't look at him. She stays at the sink.

Lizzie, Dale and Tomias come round the corner, talking. Meg signals to them to stop and be quiet.

What are you doing? Lizzie asks with a twist of her hand.

Listening to them mob, Meg answers, turning her finger to her ear and pointing with her eyebrows towards the kitchen.

Lizzie sneaks up and sits down beside Meg to listen.

Tomias sees what they're doing and walks away.

Dale stands, not sure which way to go. He wants to know about Sean but he wants to go with Tomias. 'What's happening?' he whispers. Lizzie looks at him to say, Shut up! Then she cocks her head and listens, and Dale sneaks up behind her so he can hear too.

The adults are silent. All you can hear is the rattle of cups and plates. Then Sandy starts talking. He's speaking in English so he can talk simply without making his meaning too clear.

He tells Dad the old lawman came and told him that Sean was with the old men, and that they would look after him and teach him till the water went down.

'I told them, "That boy's parents they worry for him,"' Sandy says. 'But they reckon it's time now for him to learn. They can have him back when he knows.'

Dad asks in language, 'Is he going to be all right? Will they look after him? Is he safe?'

Mum watches Sandy's face carefully to see if he will tell the truth.

He looks up at her quickly and nods.

As Sandy gets up to leave, Dad says, 'Sandy, I think maybe we shouldn't tell everyone about ...' and he stops. He can't bring himself to say that Sean might have gone into that sacred place. 'Maybe if we just say he's with the old men. That's the truth. No use making everyone angry.'

Sandy nods.

'Will you tell Mavis and Caroleena not to talk?'

Sandy nods again, and goes.

Dad sits in silence. Mum comes up behind him and wraps her arms around his neck.

Meg and Lizzie smile. Dale looks away.

'That's a relief,' says Dad. 'I thought ... God, I don't know what I thought, but he hasn't done anything stupid.'

'But it's ...' They both know how dangerous it is up there at this time of the year. Deadly snakes are out mating. The tiniest scratch can get infected and turn into a tropical ulcer, festering, eating deep into flesh, down to the bone.

'I know, but it'll be good for him in the long run,' Dad says. 'He'll be okay. He always takes his first-aid kit. He'll have snake bandages. He knows how to keep sores clean. He's got his backpack with everything in it. Bloody kid always packs enough dried food for a week. Much better prepared than us when we were young,' he says, trying to make a joke. 'Remember that time we got stuck between the Ferguson and the Edith, before Sean was born? Didn't have anything to eat. Plenty of beer. But not a scrap of food. We were doing the beer run!' He laughs. 'He'll be right, love. He's sixteen years old. Your dad was only seventeen when he came to this country, and he was stuck out here for years on his own.'

Mum nods.

'Don't worry yourself,' Dad says, patting her shoulder. 'Better get back to work.' And he goes back to the workshop.

Caroleena and Mavis come, and they go outside with Mum to sit in the soil. The kids have to scramble out from under each other and run around the corner, pretending they've just come in from playing down the road.

Mum wrings the jess round and round her wrist. Sean will be all right, she thinks. Those old men know this country, the animals, the plants, the spirits. Sandy says they're teaching him. I just hope he doesn't mean they're teaching him a lesson. What if they're keeping him because he did break the law? And instantly she sees Jardeen, her first love.

Beautiful Jardeen. He broke the law, so the old men broke him. All he and she had done was love each other. How could she not have loved him? His skin, the colour of wet charcoal, moved like silk over the curves of his muscles. He was tall and strong, he rode his horse long-legged like a Native American. And he was so wild and game. He could stand up on a galloping horse. He did everything flat out. And yet he was so gentle he could tame any animal – horse, cow, dingo.

They loved each other. But it was the wrong way. They were the wrong skin. They knew it was wrong but thought that because she was white, it would be okay. It wasn't. The old men took Jardeen away. To teach him, they said. Punish him and make him respect the law. When he came back he was broken, his eyes dull with pain, the thick scars on his arms still raw – so painful he couldn't move. He was someone else. She was sent to boarding school. He was married and moved to an out-station.

Mum holds the jess up to her cheek. Don't be silly. That's not going to happen to Sean. He hasn't broken any law. He's not being punished. Sandy would have told me if he'd done anything wrong.

Mavis touches the jess, holding her hand on it for a minute and then putting her hand in the soil. She's worried about Lucy. This mother needs much help, she thinks. It's too hard for women. They suffer to create the child and grow it up and then it's ripped away, leaving their heart broken. That boy should know better. I grew him up. Taught him properly. How can he bring such shame and suffering to his mother? It's that school. That in-town school. They the ones now that teach him wrong way. They got no respect. Her forehead is wrinkled into a frown, her eyes dark with anger. But it's done now. The old men know. Like Jardeen, Sean will learn. Jardeen is a big man now, an important man, a lawman and ceremony man. That pain and isolation made him strong. Sean too. They will work with that boy and make him a good man. Us women, we have to work with the mother, to give her help.

'We make that altar,' she says to Mum. 'Remember that one?'

'Yes. Of course.'

Caroleena nods: Good idea. She starts to sing. A soft, whispering song, her hand on Lucy's leg. Sean will be okay, she knows. Whatever has happened, that old ceremony man will fix it. He will sort it out. The vibrations of her voice lift up through the air and spread through the grey sky to Barrumbi, connecting. Up there, they're all right, she thinks, testing the vibrations of her song. It's down here that the real problem will be. How can she save the children here? That altar.

Yes, good idea, she will put something strong near the children, to keep them safe.

They get up and go inside. Mum takes everything off the corner cupboard and puts there Sean's boot and some candles, a picture of St Anthony, a cutting from a book of St Patrick to keep him safe from death adders, and her St Christopher medal. She gathers flowers, and a small bowl of rice and some incense.

Caroleena brings the very strong object – so secret it has to stay wrapped in cloth – and puts it on the altar too. Mum puts her hand on it, holds it there for a moment and moves it to the centre.

'You be good na,' Mavis tells the kids. 'Nomore humbug,' pointing to Mum. 'Leave'm working hard for that boy. Singing out for him.'

Caroleena sits down on the floor and with a curve of her hand tells the kids to come around her. She looks at each of them straight in the eye to make sure they're listening. 'You nomore go na that water,' she says. 'Stay here inside. That mandeuk outside,' she says, pointing to the rain, 'that rain, he'll get you, finish.'

She's so serious they all nod their heads.

Mum goes back to doing her work, cooking and washing. She hangs wet nappies all over the house, in the louvres, on chairs. The house is full of that Wet season smell of damp clothes and soup.

11

Wet Season Fun

The ground's saturated now and the water runs off quickly, washing the drains clean, flowing across the ground, loosening the soil and carrying it brown and murky to the creek. The creek's rushing so fast there's foam on the edges, creamy foam sprinkled with little sticks and bits of grass. Perfect for riding the tubes.

Sean's okay. Dad even said. Everyone heard him say not to worry. Even Mum's not too worried any more. She's not back to normal. You can tell because when Leroy and Susan cry she just gives them something to eat or gives them a cuddle. She doesn't tease them, telling them about the soldiers in their blood that fight all the germs when they cut themselves. But she smiles and talks a bit so everything must be all right. Anyway, Mavis mob come over every day and they go bush to bring back herbs, seeds and leaves to add to the altar; medicine plants so that Sean will remember what to use on his sores and boils, or what to eat if he gets bitten by a poisonous snake. Sean's just staying up there for a while with the old men, camping, and then he'll come home. So it's no use wasting the Wet season sitting inside. They may as well have some fun.

'Let's get some tubes and go ride the creek,' Dale says.

'Caroleena reckons to stay away from that water,' Lizzie answers.

Tomias turns his hand over to ask Dale what Caroleena said.

'Don't worry. She just hates anyone having fun. She's the one what made us go to Barrumbi,' Dale says quickly. 'None of this would have happened if she didn't make us go to Barrumbi.'

Reuben gets up and walks out. He's going home. His family's been in trouble before and he's not going there again. But he doesn't want to sound like a sook so he doesn't tell anyone.

Tomias sees him go and looks at Lizzie to find out what's happening, but before she can say anything Dale says, 'Come on Tomias. Leave them scaredy cats here.'

Dale and Tomias run down the road, Lizzie and Jimmy following. When they get close to the workshop Dale waves everybody behind him and they sneak around the wall to see who's there. Dale doesn't want to see Sandy. Caroleena will definitely have told Sandy to keep the kids away from the creek. She tells him everything.

Dad and Sandy are out the front of the workshop, sipping tea and smoking. The kids run round the back. Under some sheets of tin there are tubes waiting to be fixed.

'They got hole,' Tomias whispers.

'Doesn't matter, we'll get them patched.'

They grab the tubes, picking big ones.

'Where's the patches?'

'Under the workbench.'

'Lizzie, go talk to Dad mob so we can get the patches,' Dale says.

Lizzie looks at him. Dale's always making her do the talking. 'Why don't you?' she says, even though she knows she's the best person. If Dale went he would fumble and look guilty and stuff everything up.

'Go on Lizzie, you're the best.'

Lizzie rolls her eyes. That's better. It's so good when Dale has to admit that she's smarter than him. She tosses her head and walks around to Dad, the red pigtails that stick out the top of her hat bouncing.

Dale sneaks into the shed. Tomias and Jimmy wait, holding their breath, leaning against the shed wall, waiting, waiting, waiting.

They hear Dale rattling around inside. Quiet, Dale! Don't make so much noise.

Then it goes quiet. Completely quiet. Can't even hear Lizzie talking.

'What're youse doing around here!'

Shit! We're caught. They jump up.

Dale cracks up laughing. He shows them a handful of patches and runs past them flat out up the road. They tuck a tube under each arm and follow him to the school.

Soon the smell of sulphur fills the air in the assembly area as they light the patches to melt them over the holes in the tubes. They're nearly finished when they hear Dad's car pull up. 'What you mob doing?' he asks.

Bloody Lizzie must've told! How could she? What'm I gonna say? Shanghais. Just say we're making shanghais. But before Dale can open his mouth Lizzie comes running up. 'Just fixing tubes for the creek,' she says.

Dale looks at her hard. *Whatdja tell for!*

Lizzie looks back at Dale to say, I didn't tell. He just came past!

Dale sneers to say he doesn't believe her.

'Water might be a bit high,' says Dad.

'Nah. It's all right,' Dale says. 'We just went down there and checked – it's all right.'

'Chuck the tubes in the back of the Toyoda when you've finished,' Dad says. 'And I'll drive you down and have a look.'

No way! Dale thinks, knowing the water's fast. He'll never let them play. Never. Now their fun is spoilt. Bloody Lizzie.

They're in the back of the Toyoda. 'Whatdja tell for! I was gonna say we was making shanghais.'

'Right, Dale,' Lizzie says. 'Like you would patch a tube before you cut it into strips and make it into a shanghai.' Her face is really sarcastic. 'Do you think Dad's totally stupid?'

Dale looks away. Lizzie thinks she's so smart.

When they get to the creek Dad sits in the car watching the water. It's a bit high, but he doesn't want to stop them playing tubes. They've been hanging around the house for days. They've got to have a bit of fun with all this worry about Sean.

'Dad,' Lizzie says, interrupting his thoughts. 'Remember how you built that flying fox to get stuff across the river during the big flood? And you put a rope downstream in case anyone got swept away?'

Dad nods.

'Well, could we put a rope across the river like that?

Just to be safe. Not that it's a flood or anything, but you can't be too careful,' she says, using her most adult voice.

'Good idea,' Dad says, pulling her pigtails. 'If you stay in this area here you'll be safe.'

Dale looks at her to say, Quick thinking, good on ya Lizzie.

She looks back, lifting her eyebrows and shrugging her shoulders, her face gammon real smart.

Dad dives in and swims to the other bank to stretch a rope across the creek from tree to tree, marking out a playing area above the place where the current gets fast and dangerous. Dale and Tomias run upstream, jump in, and, lying on top of their tubes, speed down the creek.

Dad watches as they put up their hands, grab the rope and pull themselves to the bank. He nods, satisfied they'll be all right, and goes back to the workshop.

The kids run up the creek on both sides, jumping into the water and speeding down to the rope. Then they jump out and run up the bank again.

Squeals of laughter fill the air, and more kids come to play.

High above them, the escarpment is just visible behind cloud. The squeals and laughter vibrate through the moist air, up into the clouds and across the land. At the Long Hole spring the tiny particles of water that caressed Sean and wrapped themselves around Dale in Chinaman Creek are floating, weak and diluted. When they hear the children they slip over the silver waterfalls and down into the creek. The children's laughter ripples across the surface of the water, calling. The particles murmur, tingle, hesitate, listen, and move closer to the noise, hungry, alert.

'My turn,' Lizzie yells, putting her arm out to stop everyone going past. She's at the start.

'Too late!' Jimmy ducks under her arm and jumps in. But he isn't holding the tube properly and is still scrambling to get back on when he hits the water. He starts to slip off. He kicks, trying to lift himself up onto the tube, but the water around him spins and lifts, tugging the tube out from beneath him. He kicks harder, pushing the water down, but it climbs over him, pulling him under.

Lizzie's right behind him. She sees his arms waving around, his head disappearing. 'Jimmy? What're you doing?' She reaches down and grabs him by the shirt and pulls him up. Jimmy wraps his arms around her tube, his face white with fear.

'What's the matter?' she asks.

'Reeds. I think the reeds was grabbing me,' he says. 'I wanna get out.'

One on each side of Lizzie's tube, their arms holding tight, they kick really hard against the current to get to the bank and climb out.

'There's no reeds there, Jimmy.'

'I know,' he says, looking back at the water. Then he remembers his tube. 'My tube. Got to get my tube,' he yells, and runs down the bank.

'Forget it,' Lizzie yells out to him, but he doesn't hear.

*

Dale's beating everyone. He's always the quickest. He's got this little tube so he can lie on top of it and use both his hands and his legs. And he's got this special underwater kick that makes him go really fast. He looks back – there's no one. Then he sees Jimmy's tube floating down by itself and quickly spins around and swims over to grab it.

'That's mine. Give us it back,' Jimmy yells, running along the bank.

'Nah. Good as gone,' Dale says. 'If I hadn't grabbed it you'd've lost it!'

'Give us it back,' Jimmy yells, nearly crying.

Dale pulls the two tubes together and lies across both of them on his back, his body stretched out, hands behind his head, relaxing, letting the current take him down.

Jimmy's running along the bank. 'Dale!'

Dale closes his eyes. 'Wicked tube bed this one,' he says, floating along.

And goes right under the rope.

'Dale! The rope! You missed the rope!' Jimmy screams.

Dale spins around. 'The rope?'

The current's fast, taking him down towards the rapids. Dale doesn't want to lose the tubes so he tries to paddle to the bank, holding both of them, but they're too big – too bulky. The water holds them, pulling them downstream. He kicks and kicks but he just keeps going downstream, faster and faster. *Gotta let them go and swim.* He slips into the water and starts swimming, using his special really strong kick. But the water pulls his legs down. He's not getting any closer. He swims and swims, his arms aching. Jimmy runs along the bank, screaming, 'Go with it! Swim with the current! Don't fight it!', saying what everyone always tells him. But Dale can't get his legs up to kick. They keep sinking.

'Tomias, Tomias!' Jimmy yells. Tomias is just floating down on his tube, reaching up for the rope. 'Tomias, Dale's drowning!'

Tomias lets the rope go and paddles quickly downstream using his arms and legs, heading straight for Dale. Dale goes under. Tomias reaches down. Dale grabs Tomias's hand, pulls himself up onto the tube, breathing heavily, holding on tight. One on either side of the tube, they kick and kick, their feet above the surface mixing air and water to make white bubbles. The water breaks up; it can't hold them. It loses its grip and they get to the shore.

Jimmy runs up. 'You all right?'

Dale nods and looks up at him to say, Sorry about the tube.

Everyone else comes up. 'Dale! What happened?'

Dale shakes his head and shrugs his shoulders.

They're all suddenly cold. Their lips are purple. Lizzie and Tomias build a fire under the paperbarks with tiny twigs and they warm themselves in the thick dark smoke of wet wood.

Later they walk downstream to find the tubes. Maybe they're caught in a tree or something.

Nothing. There's a waterfall. The creek water pours over steps made from logs and matted roots and tumbles down the rocks into the big river.

They drag rocks to the bank and build a good fireplace

under the paperbarks. Hands extended to get warm, they sit around their fire and tell flood stories.

D'ja hear about that time one boy drowned, caught in a whirlpool? He was a real good swimmer but that water grabbed him and held him under. They never found his body. They reckon that whirlpool sucked him into a deep cave under the river.

What about that time someone was sleeping in a dry creek-bed and a flash flood washed him away? They found him up a tree, still alive, but he had no feet. He couldn't get his feet out of the water so they went all wrinkled and soft and the fish ate all his toes. He just had bones sticking out.

Or that time when a lady with a little baby girl was trying to cross a flooded creek and her baby was dragged out of her arms and washed away. The water just spun round the little girl, swirling round and round until the mother couldn't hold her any more. She loosened her grip and the water took her away. The lady went mad. That little girl was singing out to her in her dreams, 'Mummy help me. Mummy help me.'

The sky darkens behind the hills. Heavy clouds start moving fast over their heads. It starts to rain, heavy rain, wild rain, roaring at them sideways. They run home, the drops, sharp as needles, hitting their faces.

12

Things Fall Apart

It rains loudly all night. In the morning the downpour slows to a drizzle and the kids run to check out the creek. The current's really fast now; rapids and whirlpools are sucking and spinning around sunken logs. Rain starts to pour again, filling their eyes with water, rushing past them in a torrent and loosening the dirt under their feet.

'Come on, let's go.' They run back to the school and hang out in the assembly area, throwing tennis balls at the walls.

Next day it's still raining. The creek's up, right above the rope and the fireplace. It's lapping around the paper-bark trunks. The young trees in the creek-bed bend over, swaying. Water swirls around the big trees, washing the soil from under them. Dale, Lizzie, Jimmy and Tomias wander down to the river again.

The waterfalls are gone. There's a mass of water pouring over the rocks. The river's wide; big logs and branches float past, snakes, bandicoots, rats and goannas draped over them, wet and frightened. A dead dog is caught between two trees – bloated, stinking, its eye sockets empty.

'That'll bring the crocs up,' Tomias reckons.

A sharp bark echoes from downstream.

'Hear that?' Lizzie says. It's crocs calling to each

other, marking their new territories as they move up the river. But if you hear a croc you don't talk about it or they will hear you and think you are teasing them, so Tomias just says, 'What?'

It starts to rain again. It's not right, this rain, Lizzie thinks. It's like the rain at Barrumbi – too heavy. It just keeps raining and raining; drizzling for half an hour like a dripping tap and then full bore again.

And then a watery murmur floats on the air. The murky water in the big river starts to call them. The longer they stand on the bank the more they feel it calling them: Come, come. They watch the water flowing past, slick and smooth, floating along, easy. They could just lie on its surface and ride downstream, all the way to the sea. Easy. Just float along.

'I'm going,' Lizzie reckons.

'Yeah. Boring here.'

They run down the road to the workshop, jumping over puddles, kicking the muddy water high in the air.

There's heaps of people in the workshop. Must be big meeting. Lots of old people milling outside in the rain listening – someone inside yelling in language.

The kids walk closer.

Go away! the old people outside say to them with a sharp wave of their hands. Go away. This is not your business.

They sneak around behind the workshop and climb up on the old drums to peek over the wall.

Dad and Sandy are sitting, heads down.

One old man's yelling at them, waving a spear,

threatening to hit them with his fighting stick. He's yelling about water, the river; something bad's happening – maybe a flood, maybe someone will die. He's really angry because Dad and Sandy didn't tell him what happened at Barrumbi – that Sean got lost up there near Death Adder Ridge. The old man says that he might have been able to do something to stop the flood if he'd known what happened. But now it's too late. All this rain, he says. Your family caused this problem. You causing this trouble.

Then he stops yelling. You tell us now! he says in sign language to Sandy. You tell us what happened. And he waits, leaning on his spear.

Dad keeps his head down.

Sandy talks in Mayali language so Dad can understand what he says. He tells the old man what happened at Barrumbi. About that eldest child for Lucy, daughter of the old man who came here, the old man, white man who built the station. His daughter and her children still live here. 'All this time,' he says, pointing to Dad, 'they live here. Grown up here now.' He says that old man's grandson went missing when they went to Barrumbi. Sandy says how he and Dad went back but they couldn't get through. How he went in the helicopter, was dropped off at Barrumbi and walked to the Death Adder escarpment. He lit a fire and waited all day till one of the old lawmen came to meet him. The old lawman said that they had that white boy there, teaching him.

'What's that boy doing there! Who let him go there? Why doesn't he know?' one old man says in language.

'Maybe the lawmen took him there,' Sandy says.

The old man looks hard at him to say, You know that's not true, and someone outside yells, 'Bullshit!' and something else in another language so that Dad can't understand.

Caroleena walks into the workshop with her stick. She pulls her big body up really tall and straight. 'He's got respect that boy, biggest son for Lucy, grandson for that old man. He subbie. He doesn't go there.'

'You can't talk,' the old man says. He turns his head away from her to say, You the one now that took these people to Barrumbi. You the one now to blame for this trouble.

Everything's quiet. Just the rain tinkling on the tin roof.

Then Dad starts talking, his voice quiet and respectful to the old man. He says that maybe it's just a big water Wet season – it happens many times and he names the ones he remembers, like the year Leroy was born and when Dale was born. The community was cut off for months by big water that year. Nobody had done anything wrong. People often get caught by the Wet season. Last year three men from Opium Creek station got stuck up in the escarpment for two months. They hadn't done anything wrong. They just waited there till the water went down, and then they came home.

The old man turns his face away from Dad, not wanting to listen to him. It's not just the rain and the rising water, you silly man, he thinks. It's the air. It's things you'll never understand. Something's wrong. But he doesn't say anything. He's finished with talking now. Nobody knows what happened yet. They just have to wait and see, then they'll take revenge if necessary. He looks at Sandy to say, It'll be your fault, yours and Caroleena's, when something bad happens, and he walks out of the workshop.

The kids sneak away. They don't talk about what they've heard. It's too hard. Sean is Dale and Jimmy and Lizzie's brother. The old man is Tomias's relative. Mavis and Caroleena are in trouble. Is it their fault or Sean's? If it's Sean's fault, then it's Dale and Jimmy and Lizzie's fault too. They might get punished.

Tomias shouldn't be with Dale mob. He knows that now. Everyone should leave them alone, ignore them until the trouble is over. That must be why Reuben left that day. Why he's been hanging around at home.

'Gotta go you mob,' he says quickly, and takes off down a little track through the clinic yard.

'Tomias? Wait!' Dale yells. But Tomias disappears through the gap in the fence and around the corner of the kitchen, leaving Dale behind.

The kids stop and watch him go. The three of them alone on the wide wet road. Then the wind whips up a cool breeze from under the grey clouds, and suddenly they're cold, goosebumps sticking up all over their skin, and they run home.

Mum's listening to the radio, the weather report. The voices of local station owners and policemen crackle along the line. *Pushed all the stock up into high ground … One old man missing … Clara's gonna have her kid – have to send in a helicopter to take her to town … Should get everyone up into the school … More rain coming.*

Mum's face is worried.

'Mum, can we light the stove?' Lizzie asks.

'Yeah,' Mum says without looking.

They stand around the small fire in the wood stove, drinking warm milk, making toast on the top and covering it with sugarbag honey to warm their jittery bellies.

Tomias left us, Dale thinks. It's not even night time. Does he reckon it's our fault too? Or worse, is everyone going to ignore us mob now? Will I have to walk around alone like Reuben did that time when his mother got in trouble? Everyone turning their faces away when he walked past. No one letting him eat at their place.

'Do you reckon that old man's talking about that flood spirit?' Lizzie whispers. 'You know, that one Mavis told us when we were little. That one what hunts for warm animals and sucks ya blood and stuff? So ya go all like grey and soft?'

'That's just a kids' story to keep ya away from the water.'

'But if it's that spirit, it will stay flooding till someone dies. Till that spirit gets itself a human body,' Lizzie goes on.

Silence.

'What'd it feel like, Jimmy? When you was in the water?' Lizzie asks.

'Just reeds,' Jimmy says. He doesn't want to say that it felt as if the water was dragging him, pulling him under. Dale will laugh at him.

'Like hands or something?'

Jimmy shakes his head.

'Dale!' Lizzie says. 'What was it like?'

'I don't know,' Dale says, annoyed, but he shudders, remembering feeling the cold – coldness like fingers caressing his legs, seducing them into stillness, sucking onto their warmth. Shame job. He's not talking about that in front of everyone.

'Anyway, we should have listen to Caroleena,' Lizzie says, looking at Dale as if it's his fault.

Dale rolls his eyes at her.

'Where's Tomias?' Mum asks, coming into the kitchen. But when she sees the mess they're making, dripping sugarbag on the top of the stove, she doesn't wait for an answer. 'Look at this! Clean that up! You'll stink the house out.'

'Just warming it up so it goes runny,' Jimmy says.

'It'll burn! Dale, get the cloth.'

But Dale isn't listening. He's worried. What about Tomias? What if he stays away? What if we can't be friends ever again?

Slap! Mum hits him across the shoulder. 'Dale! Stop daydreaming and get the cloth.'

Tomias gets home with the wind at his back and a storm thundering down around him. Reuben's there, making a spearhead out of an old piece of pipe. He's putting it in the cooking fire on the veranda till it's really hot and smashing it with a hammer on a rock. Tomias sits and watches him. He wants to ask him why he left Dale's place the other day. Why he's not hanging around with them mob, why he didn't come to the creek. But Reuben's mother always shows off about Reuben being good at school. She reckons he's smarter than everyone, especially his cousin Tomias. So Tomias can't ask him questions. It would be like admitting that Reuben's the smartest.

Mavis and Caroleena are sitting outside under the veranda so everyone can see them and know they're not ashamed. A neighbour's having a card game, but they don't join in.

Tomias gets bored. He runs up to the workshop through the rain and sits with his biggest brother Rex and Sandy. They don't talk – just sitting, thinking. Tomias wants to ask them what to do. Ask them what that old man was talking about. Why should someone die? Does he have to ignore Dale mob or is it okay to still be friends?

Then Dale's dad runs in from his car, stomping to shake the water from his raincoat and his hat. Sandy and Rex go to meet him. They treat him like normal.

They not ignoring him. It must be all right then.

Tomias smiles and gets up. He hesitates for a second, watching the grey wall of water, then he bolts through the rain, round past the kitchen, through the gap in the fence, his hand touches the star picket as he leaps the old station fence and he runs straight through the back door of Dale's place.

Tomias. Dale's face almost breaks in half, he's smiling so much. He runs at Tomias, grabs him and wrestles him to the floor, laughing. They smash into a chair, knocking it over, spreading mud and water all over the floor.

'Get out of here!' Mum yells.

They roll under the table to get away from her and she grabs the broom. 'Go on, play rough outside or I'll donk you.' She gammon swings the broom at them. They scramble to their feet and bolt out the door.

They pause, not sure what to do. It's pouring with rain – can't go anywhere.

Dale opens the door a crack. 'We'll clean up the mess, Mum.'

'Go away! I'm sick of you kids fighting and running amok in the house. Go play in the assembly area.'

'But Mum, we're cold,' Dale says in his most pathetic voice. 'Freezing and wet.' He grins at Tomias to say, That will get her.

Mum sneaks her head out the door, smiling. 'You're too cheeky, Dale. Grab the mop and come and clean this mess up,' she says.

They stand around the wood stove, eating.

'This rain's all wrong, you mob. It definitely is that spirit, like that old man said,' Lizzie says, really serious. 'We gotta stay away from the water.'

'I'm not going near no water for the rest of me life,' Jimmy says.

'Dale and Tomias?'

'What?'

'We gotta stay away from the water.'

They both look at her like she's stupid. 'As if we don't know that!'

'Good. Because if we stay away like we are meant to, the rain should stop,' she says.

Dale rolls his eyes to Tomias to say, She thinks she knows everything.

*

Outside the clouds are so thick, the rain so heavy, the sun sets in a dull grey light. It's dark at six o'clock. All through the night the old people sing. Tomias sits with his relatives and lets the music wash over him, the clapsticks sharp against his chest, the didgeridoo filling his body. The music sneaks up into Dale's house and through the louvres into his bedroom, muffled by the moist Wet season air.

Lizzie's glad the old people are singing to stop the rain. She crosses her fingers and her legs and makes wishes – 'Please make the rain stop. Please make the rain stop' – to help them.

Jimmy falls asleep straight away, exhausted, but Dale tosses and turns. In his dreams no one has a face and he's running, running, running, looking for Tomias, looking for Mavis, but everyone is no one, the world is empty.

13
The Worst Christmas

But the singing doesn't work. Nothing works. It keeps on raining for days and days and days. Roads are flooded right across the Territory. The creek cuts off the causeway. No one can get in or out of the community.

And it's Christmas day the day after tomorrow.

'What about Christmas? What about presents?' Dale says with a sudden shock.

'Not getting any,' Tomias says.

'We can make Christmas presents!' Jimmy says.

The others look at him as if to say, Yeah, like we want homemade Christmas presents!

'Wish Miss Wilson was here,' Lizzie says.

Everyone looks at her, shocked. Miss Wilson is their schoolteacher. She's gone down south for the holidays, back to her home in country Victoria. Thank God! All she ever does is stop people having fun. She's got these really blue eyes that can see through walls. You can't get away with anything in her class. And if she hangs around in the holidays she's always saying things like, 'That's dangerous,' 'Don't swim in the creek,' 'Don't go up the spring. There might be snakes up there.'

'Oh yes, wouldn't it be lovely to have Miss Wilson here,' Dale says, gammon real sarcastic. 'Yeah! 'Cause she can help us make recycled Christmas presents out of egg cartons and old milk crates. That would be fun.'

'No! She would get us proper Christmas presents,' Lizzie says. 'She would probably organise the army to get Christmas presents dropped from a chopper!'

But Dale's on a roll. 'Lizzie, you can have a money box shaped like a pig made from a balloon. Tomias, you can have the little fairy made from a toilet roll. Dale, oh Dale, you are going to love this; you can have this mobile. Look, it's made out of an egg carton,' he says, talking like Miss Wilson.

'Shuddup Dale,' Lizzie says.

'We could make something for Mum and Dad,' Jimmy reckons.

'Yeah!' Lizzie agrees.

'Like what? I know! Lizzie could shut up for a month,' Dale says, enjoying being sarcastic.

'Or you could stop being a dickhead for a week!' Lizzie says.

'Get outside, you kids,' Mum yells.

'It's wet!'

'Come here.' She grabs garbage bags and makes them all raincoats, with small white plastic shopping bags for hats. 'Stay away from the river. Go play in the assembly area. Go see your father. I don't care where you go. Just get out and stop whingeing and fighting in here!'

Dale and Tomias walk around the community, bored, slowly making their way down to the swollen creek. The raging water pours past them, carrying sticks and logs down to the river. They only stay a minute and then go back up past the workshop. They look in the kitchen, see who's playing in the assembly area. No one. They're happy when it starts to rain again and they've got an excuse to go home.

Mum has pulled the Christmas decorations out of the linen cupboard; they're spread all over the table. 'It's not going to be much of a Christmas, I'm afraid,' she says.

'It'll be right,' Lizzie answers, starting to sort through the decorations. They're the same Christmas decorations they've had for years. The line of white snowmen cut from a long strip of paper with cotton wool for snow and red nail polish for buttons. All those streamers from the year when Mum was having Leroy. The green cardboard kangaroo card Dale made when he was little – it's got 'To MUM and DAD with love' on it in the teacher's writing and Dale's name printed backwards in his Grade One writing. Dale picks up another card, one with Sean's little handprints on it – the one he made in preschool. *These are my hands, So tiny and small. Watch them grow, Till I am tall.* He slips it quickly under the others so Mum doesn't see.

'We won't be able to get a proper Christmas tree,' Lizzie says. 'We'll have to cut the top off our cypress pine to decorate. We can't get over the river to get one from Christmas Creek.'

Mum looks at her, her eyebrows raised.

'Just the top. It would grow again.'

'See what Dad finds. He said he'd have a look around.'

*

When Dad comes home they cut off the top of the cypress pine and put it in an old flour drum with stones in the bottom. Standing on chairs, Meg and Mum hang decorations on the tree. Dale and Tomias hand up the decorations and Lizzie says where the spaces are. Meg and Jeweleen make little cups out of gumnuts with birthday candles in them and put them all over the branches. Dad climbs the ladder and puts the star right up the top.

On Christmas eve they sit in the lounge room and Mum tries to be happy singing Christmas songs. Even Dale and Tomias join in when they sing the chorus of 'Rudolph the Red-Nosed Reindeer'.

'Can we open our presents at midnight? It's Christmas then!' Jimmy says.

'We haven't got any presents, Jimmy. We haven't been able to get to town.'

Everyone's quiet. Could it be true they're not going to get anything?

'As soon as the creek goes down we'll go to town and buy you whatever you want, but you're going to have to wait.'

Lizzie doesn't believe it. She's sure she can see a smirk under Mum's serious face. So, early on Christmas morning, when it's still dark outside, she sneaks out, tiptoes past Mum and Dad's room, to look under the Christmas tree. Mum always has presents stashed away in the linen cupboard, little things, surprises for birthdays if someone comes to stay. She knows there's no way Mum would make her kids go without Christmas presents. No way.

But there's nothing under the tree. Just the empty

decoration boxes. The stockings aren't even out as they should be, hanging along the louvres, all filled with lollies and liquorice. There's nothing anywhere. Lizzie stands and stares – she can't believe her eyes.

It's silent outside but soon the birds will start to sing and everyone will wake up on this, the worst Christmas day in the world. Lizzie's shoulders slump. She's walking softly down the hall to go back to bed when she bumps into Jimmy. 'Oh!' he says.

'Don't bother,' Lizzie says. 'No use looking, there's nothing.'

'Really? That's not fair.'

'Shhh! Don't wake up Mum and Dad.'

'But?'

'Well, they can't help it if it's a flood.'

'It's not raining.'

They stop and listen. It's not raining! Lizzie opens the door and steps outside. There are no stars, so the sky must still be covered with clouds, but the air is fresh and light. Maybe the big rain is over. The kids have stayed away from the water since the big meeting. Every night the old people have sung and done business. Lizzie has wished and begged and pleaded. Maybe it's worked, she thinks. Oh, wouldn't it be good if the rain's stopped! The creek would go down. It does go down really quick! And we could go to town and get presents. And have a proper Christmas.

Jimmy's in the lounge room. Nothing! He can't believe it! Mum must be so embarrassed. He looks through the louvres. 'No presents,' he whispers to Lizzie. 'Nothing!'

Lizzie goes back inside. 'Told ya.'

They sit down on the floor on the cushions and smell that special Christmas smell of cypress pine inside the house.

'Hey,' Lizzie says. 'We should make Mum and Dad breakfast in bed!'

'Yeah! Banana pikelets!'

They close the hallway door, turn on the light in the kitchen to find all the ingredients.

'No bananas!'

'Any eggs?'

'Nah, the chook pen's all wet and the chooks are turned off laying.'

'What can we make?'

'Baked beans?' Jimmy says, looking in the pantry.

'Yeah, what about baked beans on toast with melted cheese and chilli! Dad would love that!' Lizzie says.

They toast one side of the bread under the grill, then spoon baked beans on the untoasted side, top it with cheese and put it back under the grill to melt.

'What about coffee?'

'Yeah. Dad loves coffee. Put the beans on toast in the oven or they'll get cold.'

They make a coffee. 'How many?' Jimmy asks, holding up a tablespoon.

'I think it's like Milo – a couple of big ones.'

When everything's ready Lizzie puts it all on a tray. 'I'll carry it,' she says. 'You get the door.'

They open the bedroom door and turn on the light. Mum and Dad are still asleep, the two of them crushed together on Dad's side, Dad's arm over Mum's waist, little Susan stretched out in a star shape on Mum's side, taking up most of the bed.

Quickly Jimmy turns off the light and he and Lizzie back out. Through the hallway louvres they see it's still dark – dead dark. 'It's still night time.' They look at each other and giggle. 'What we gonna do?'

'Eat it?' Jimmy says, a sparkle in his eyes.

'Nah, not enough cheese to make more. We can drink the coffee.'

Mum never lets them have coffee, so this is going to be fun.

They put the baked beans in the oven to keep warm and sit near the Christmas tree to wait and drink the coffee.

It's disgusting!

'Wonder why Dad likes it?' Jimmy asks. Dad always drinks coffee in the morning. Why, when it's so yucky?

Down at middle camp Caroleena hears the rain stop. It has slowed down to a tinkle on the roof before, but this is the first time in more than a week it has really stopped. Not a drop. Absolute silence. She lies awake, her body alert, her heart beating faster with hope. Her old dog senses she's awake and comes in, putting his cold nose under the sheet to say, Hello, what's wrong?

She stays silent. If something good is happening, best not to talk about it. She climbs out of bed, pushes the big log on the fire awake, gives it some small sticks to keep it going and puts the billy on. Her other dogs come to greet her. 'Get out you mob. No more humbug,' she says.

She goes to the windowsill and selects a little brown ball of mabutj, chewing tobacco she makes from special tobacco leaves and white ash from a clean fire. Folding her skirt between her legs, she sits down beside the fire, her back straight, her legs crossed beneath her, and puts the mabutj ball in her mouth between her lip and teeth. It sticks out like a big lump on one side. Slowly the saliva softens it and the bitterness oozes out into her mouth. 'Mmm.' She nods, and closes her eyes. Now she can think.

The sky lightens around her as the sun comes up, turning the clouds pink and orange. This is good, she thinks, the children have stayed away from the water, it has not tasted them, now it will go away.

She gets up and walks along the road down to bottom camp, a line of dogs following, their shapes silhouetted against the orange sunlight.

Lizzie and Jimmy wait and wait. They nearly fall asleep with waiting. But just when the sky starts to grey they hear little Susan wake up. They race into the kitchen to make more coffee and take the tray of food to Mum and Dad.

This time Mum's awake, sitting up in bed feeding Susan. 'Happy Christmas,' Lizzie and Jimmy say, climbing up on the bed. Dad wakes up, his eyebrows frowning, hand up to stop the light hurting his half-asleep eyes. 'What's going on?' he says.

'The kids have made us breakfast in bed for Christmas,' Mum says.

He tries to smile, sitting up and leaning back on the

pillows against the louvres, and has a slurp of his coffee. His face twists up against the bitter taste. 'Oh,' he says. 'Needs a bit more milk, love.' He hands it back to Lizzie.

'We made baked-beans-on-top-of-toast,' Lizzie says, handing him the plate.

Dad takes a bite and the baked beans run down his chin. He quickly pulls the plate in to stop them falling on the sheet and *tip!* all the baked beans slop off the toast and onto the plate.

Everyone looks at Dad, their smiles hidden. Will he get cranky? He does get cranky in the morning sometimes.

Dad is still for a moment, looking at the beans on the plate and the soggy toast in his hand. Then a grin lifts the corner of his mouth. 'Baked-beans-off-of-toast,' he says, and everyone laughs.

Lizzie and Jimmy sit on the end of the bed talking and talking – making sure they don't embarrass Mum by mentioning Christmas presents. Little Leroy wakes up and crawls onto Lizzie's lap, his eyes sleepy. 'Whatcha doing?'

'It's Christmas, Leroy!' Mum says.

'Oh,' he says, and closes his eyes, too tired.

Soon the others are awake too. Everybody sits on Mum and Dad's bed, telling stories and laughing. Then Dad says, 'Come on you kids. Need your help down the workshop.'

'Oh, *Dad*! It's Christmas day!'

'There's work to be done nevertheless!'

14

The Rain Stops

The sun is out. It's hot and steamy. The sky is the brightest blue, and puffy white clouds drift across it as calm as calm can be. Mum, Dad and the little kids get in the front of the Toyoda. Dale, Lizzie, Jimmy and Meg lie in the back, their eyes closed against the glare, feeling the warmth on their faces and their skin. It's lovely.

When they arrive at the workshop everyone's there, waiting. Dale jumps out of the car and runs to Tomias. 'What's going on? Get any presents?'

'Nothing,' Tomias says, like he's only gammon. Bet Mavis got him something and he's too embarrassed to say 'cause he knows Dale got nothing.

'Dale and Tomias!' Dad yells. 'Come in here and give us a hand.'

'Bet we're the only kids in the world who have to work on Christmas day,' Dale says, walking slowly behind Tomias into the workshop.

And he sees it! A pontoon! A huge pontoon made out of forty-four-gallon drums with a trampoline welded on top.

He spins around to Tomias. 'You knew!'

'Just now. Sandy showed us mob just now.'

'Wow!'

'Shaggy! This is the best, Dad!'

'Not just me, Sandy and Rex too.'

'Thanks! Wow!' Meg says. 'This is the best Christmas present in the world!' She gives Dad and then Sandy the biggest hugs, making them laugh with embarrassment.

'We bags first go!' Dale yells, running over, climbing up and sitting legs spread in the middle of the trampoline. The best thing about Sean not being here is that we can get the best spots, he thinks. If Sean was here, he would just push us out of the way and take over. But he's not here. So me and Tomias are first.

A guilty thought slips into Dale's mind, telling him he should be missing Sean, not happy that he's gone. But the other kids yell, 'No way, we're first too!' and climb up on the trampoline to claim their space, so he gets distracted.

'There's plenty of room. No need to fight!' says Dad, and then, smiling at Sandy and Rex, 'Let's get the bloody thing out of here before they start a riot.'

They get the Toyoda and trailer and back it up to the workshop. Kids and dogs climb all over the pontoon, running between the car and the trailer, nearly getting run over. Mum and Mavis yell at the kids to get out of the way but they can't hear them. Heaps of people have come up to watch and shout instructions: 'This way!' 'This way! 'Look out!' Dad goes red in the face and yells at the kids, '*Get off!*' He jumps out of the car and runs at them, his arm raised, his tongue folded over to show he's really angry. Kids scatter, killing themselves laughing.

Finally the car and the trailer with the huge pontoon on it move down the road. All the kids run along beside it, so excited.

'Hey, where's Reuben?' Lizzie asks.

'Home.'

'Why?'

'Makin' stuff,' Tomias says, although everyone knows it's not true.

He's probably worried about the spirit water, Lizzie thinks. And at that moment she sees the water in the billabong, wide and creamy, lapping right up near the paperbarks. 'What about that water thing?' she whispers to Dale, and hangs back.

Jimmy stops too, waiting with her. He's not going near any water ever again.

But everyone's so excited it's hard for Dale to stop and think. 'That was creek water,' he yells back to them. 'The creek water comes down from Barrumbi. This's the billabong.'

Maybe that's true, Lizzie thinks. The billabong and the creek water don't mix until the creek's real flooded. The spirit water that dragged them down in the creek came from Barrumbi. If the creek and the billabong haven't joined up yet it wouldn't be able to get in here.

'Come on you mob!' Dad yells. 'Give us a hand! Get a bloody move on!'

Then they have to go. What would they tell Dad? That Dale and Jimmy nearly drowned, and they reckon it was a spirit in the water trying to kill them, and they never told anyone?

They try to keep on the dry side, but with everyone else pushing and pulling they end up knee-deep in mud. The pontoon goes out onto the water, and it floats! They put it on the edge of the billabong so the water is shallow on one side and deep on the other. In no time the pontoon is covered with bodies. Tomias gets on. He bounces high on the trampoline, right up in the sky, and dives off into the deep-water side.

He swims back.

It must be okay, Dale thinks. He jumps high, holding his breath, closing his eyes, and *splash!* the water closes in over him. Down, down he goes till his feet touch the bottom, and up he bounces, up into the light, water spraying out from him in silver drops.

'It's okay!' he yells to Lizzie, swimming back.

Jimmy's watching from the bank. The sun sparkles on the water and the wet bodies. All them little kids – what if one of them drowns, he thinks, looking back over his shoulder at the adults. They don't seem worried. Maybe it's true the spirit water can't get to the billabong. Caroleena is sitting under a tree. He runs over to her. She's splitting pandanus leaves into long thin strands and rubbing them on her leg to make string. Her fingernails are long and hard, the pandanus white against her dark hands. Jimmy sits beside her.

She touches his worried little face, lifting her eyebrows to ask him what's wrong.

He shrugs his shoulders.

'You right. Mightbe all right,' she says.

Jimmy looks at her. She doesn't know about the creek. How they didn't listen to her and they went and played and nearly got drowned. So she can't make a good decision. But what about all the other kids playing at the creek? How come them and Tomias never got sucked under? Maybe that spirit only wants Sean's family. What about Lizzie and Dale? He stands up and looks. They're jumping in and swimming around. It must be all right. But still he doesn't want to chance it, so he stays by Caroleena, stripping the tiny spikes off the edges of the pandanus leaves.

'This one,' she says. 'I make you dilly bag, Jimmy?'

Jimmy smiles. That would be so cool. 'For green plum ...'

'You subbie.' Caroleena smiles, leaning her huge body over to snuggle against him. 'And that white currant him ready soon, bush apple red one.'

Dale and Tomias try to kick everyone else off the pontoon. 'We bagged first go!'

'We didn't agree, so tough!' Lizzie yells back.

Dale and Tomias jump and jump on the trampoline, higher and higher, dangerously close to the other kids, trying to scare them. The little kids try to crawl out of the way but can't, because they keep getting bounced up and down. They're crying.

'Get out, Dale! *Dad! Dad!* I'm telling!'

But Mum and Dad have gone back in the Toyoda to get some food. Mavis, Caroleena and all the other adults are up sitting under the paperbarks. Someone has made a fire. They have a billy on and people are coming from everywhere with flour and meat to cook. They ignore the kids.

Meg yells at Dale and Tomias, 'Stop it! You're going to hurt someone!'

'Well, get off and you won't be hurt!' Dale answers back.

'Just sit on ya knees!' Lizzie yells.

Meg, Jeweleen and Lizzie all sit on their knees, taking the shock out of the bounce by rocking up and back.

'Come on,' Lizzie says to the little kids. 'Sit like this. Don't be frighten.'

Soon there are heaps of kids all kneeling around the edge of the trampoline holding hands. It's fun. But best of all Tomias and Dale can't bounce high – the weight of all the other kids has taken the bounce out of the mat.

'You're too fat!' Dale says to the girls.

But they just laugh back and eventually he and Tomias have to give up.

'Youse can't even use it properly,' Dale says. Him and Tomias could jump higher and higher and bounce into the air and do somersaults or back flips into the water. What are that mob going to do? Just jump off and climb back up. What a waste!

'Let's take turns,' Meg says. And they do for a while, but Dale and Tomias get sick of waiting. They want to do something else. Then Tomias remembers the old tin canoe. They made it last year in the workshop, turning up the sides of a piece of tin, knocking over the sharp edges with pliers and a hammer. They spent hours paddling around the billabong, catching fish, sneaking up really close to ducks, raiding goose nests. 'Let's get the canoe,' he says.

'Yeah, stuff this mob,' Dale answers.

They run back up to Dale's house, around the side, and it's still there. Yes! Under the mango tree where they left it. Tomias turns it over. One paddle's been eaten by white-ants.

'S'all right,' Dale reckons, not wanting to waste time making another. 'One'll do.' They patch up the rust holes with chewing-gum and carry the canoe down to the billabong, holding it on their heads with both hands.

They take it around to the other side of the billabong where no one can hassle them. The water is so still the sunlight bounces off it and they have to squint their eyes almost closed. Little spear-shaped waterlily leaves are pushing up to the surface. When they make it to the top they spread across the water, flat and waxy. Some curl up crinkly at the edges and hold drops of water in round silver balls like mercury. Jesus birds walk over the lily pads, spreading their long toes across the whole leaf to stay afloat.

Dale and Tomias paddle out and watch the flocks of birds: whistling ducks, magpie geese and Burdekin ducks with their so-white breasts stark against their jet-black bodies.

'They mate for life,' Tomias reckons. 'One time there was two Burdekin ducks in that chook pen. You know that kid from town, he killed one. With a shanghai. That other one sitdown, sitdown. It died poor thing.'

The sun is warm on their backs and the billabong quiet except for the screeches of waterbirds and squeals of the kids playing right over the other side. A flock of ducks takes off, legs running across the water, wings making wind ripples on the surface. Others are coming in to land, their broad flat feet skidding to a stop, their wings wide, flap-flapping, their necks stretched out in greeting. Then they fold their wings and sit like balloons on the water, yabber-yabbering or ducking under so all you can see is tails and feet up in the air.

'That how come they're called ducks,' Dale says, laughing.

'Duck!' Tomias yells, gammon punching Dale.

Dale ducks.

'Got ya!'

Lizzie, Meg and Jeweleen watch Dale and Tomias peacefully canoeing in the middle of the billabong.

Lizzie points her head towards them. 'We should give them a fright.'

'Yeah. Come on,' Jeweleen says.

Quietly they slip into the water. Lizzie pulls up some waterlily stems, breaking off the leaves and sucking the stems to find ones they can breathe through.

She gives Meg and Jeweleen one each. Sucking air through the stems, the three of them swim through the murky water, staying near the surface where it's clear. Their arms stretch out in front of them and pull the water back behind them so they don't make any ripples on the surface. They slip between the waterlily stems, trying not to disturb them.

Soon they can see the shape of the tin canoe. They swim straight for it. They're going to tip it up, toss the boys out, give them the biggest fright ever.

Just then Dale and Tomias start looking for fish. They lean over the edge of the canoe, putting their faces right into the water, curling their hands around their eyes to stop the sun's reflection so they can see all the fish swimming past.

Tomias sees little black bream. You can tell they're black bream because they're always hunting, like sharks looking for prey. Archer fish spit arrows of water into the air and hit insects on the wing. There should be those, what-it-call, bort, he thinks, putting his head farther under so he can look right around. They should be hatched now, eating, getting fat. When the waterlilies are ready to flower, him and Dale catch them on little hooks, with tiny pieces of meat. They're yummy. Cooked on the coals with a little bit of salt. His belly mumbles as he thinks about it.

Tomias looks weird under the water. His face is distorted and swollen, covered with silver where millions of tiny bubbles cling to his skin.

The girls are getting closer, closer, being really careful not to make any noise. Lizzie's in front; a tight smile of anticipation pulls her lips into a thin line. The waterlily stem in her mouth curves back behind her like a long snake. The canoe's right there. Just wait for that mob. We got to get together to push and tip it over. She looks around. There's Meg and Jeweleen. She waves her hand to them, pointing to the canoe. She looks back and *there's a huge face floating in the water. Eyes wide open! Dead!* Someone's dead, floating in the billabong! A scream bubbles out of her mouth. She jerks backwards, kicking hard to get away.

Tomias is watching the little fish nibbling bits of algae from lily stems when a huge dark shape comes straight towards him. '*Croc!*' he screams underwater, '*Yakki!*', and he jumps back into the canoe, falling over onto Dale's side, his legs up in the air. The canoe tips over. They're in the water. Under the water! Tomias's eyes are wide trying to see the croc. He feels around for Dale, pulls him up by the shirt. 'Got to get out!' he yells and swims flat out for the shore.

Lizzie's choking. Her nose is full of water. Can't breathe. Light! Gotta go up. She looks for the light but can't see anything. She kicks out, swims and swims to get away, but she's going down, down, her hands outstretched.

An underground river moves between the creek and the billabong. The hungry water slips along with this river, through the silt and sand, searching, searching. It finds and holds yabby skins and dead worms. It sucks the sharp bones of fish and polishes their glassy eyes with its caresses. It moves through the black silt; up along the reeds it goes, over beetles and snails, getting tiny bits of pleasure from their cold, slow life. Then Lizzie's hot hand rushes past, pushing the reeds, vibrating the water. And suddenly the water's alive. Clouds of silt burst up from the depths, wrapping her up, lying heavy on top of her, taking her down, down. The tangle of weeds binds her arms, holding.

Meg and Jeweleen burst out of the water. 'Where's the canoe? Where's Lizzie!'

'You sunk our boat!' Dale yells, his eyes angry. 'You sunk our boat!'

'Where's Lizzie?' Meg screams, and she dives down. Nothing, there's nothing in the milky darkness.

She pops up out of the water. 'I can't find Lizzie!' She dives down again, straight down, deep. There's a shape, a dark shape. Lizzie! Upside down, her legs kicking! Meg swims down, her hands pushing the water back, till she reaches Lizzie's kicking feet. She grabs one leg, reefing it backwards, up towards the light. Jeweleen dives down to help, pulling Lizzie's head up and out into the air. Lizzie's choking. Her nose is full of water. Can't breathe, her eyes are wet, she can't see. 'Where's the dead man?'

'What?'

'What happened?' Jeweleen asks.

'Dead man floating. I saw a dead face. Eyes open, floating,' Lizzie says, gasping for breath. 'Where's Tomias?'

'*Get out! Get out you mob!*' Tomias yells from the shore. '*Croc! Crocodile! Ginga!*'

Without another word the three of them spin around and swim for the shore, nearly walking on water.

They slosh through the mud, stomping on the leaves of the yellow and white waterlilies and squashing the water chestnuts. 'Where's the croc?' Meg asks, running to dry ground.

Tomias isn't sure now if it was a croc. It was something dark moving through the water. But if it was a croc it would have got someone for sure. He says nothing.

'You sunk our canoe!' Dale yells at the girls.

'You can get the canoe when the billabong dries up,' Meg says, trying to make peace.

'It'll be totally rusted then! You girls always have to stuff up everyone's fun!' Dale yells.

'Bullshit! We didn't even touch it!' Lizzie answers.

'It's sunk!'

'You tipped it over yourself!' And then she remembers. 'I saw a face. A dead face in the water.'

'What?'

'I saw a dead face in the water.'

Silence.

Then Dale laughs. 'That was me and Tomias, you idiot,' he says. 'We was looking in the water for fish. *I saw a dead face*,' he says, his voice copying Lizzie's.

The mud beneath their feet is black, stinking of rotting vegetation. Lizzie kicks it up, spraying it at Dale. 'Just shuddup Dale!' she yells.

He reaches down and grabs a handful and throws it at her, splatting it across her turned back.

Her face pink with anger, she dives at Dale, knocking him over, wrestling him to the ground, rubbing mud all through his hair and his eyes.

He is laughing so much he can't fight her. '*I saw a dead face*,' he keeps saying in a squeaky scared voice.

'Say sorry,' she yells.

'Sorry Lizzie, sorry,' Dale laughs. 'It wasn't you what drowned our canoe. It was the crocodile monster and the dead face man.'

Lizzie and Dale are rolling around in the mud, both of them laughing now. Everything is going to be okay. To think anything else would be madness. It hasn't rained all day. The sky above them is light blue; thick white clouds hang there making weird shapes. Two more days like this and the creek will fall. They'll go to town to buy Christmas presents. Sean and the old men will be able to get out and come home.

Over on the other side of the billabong the kids are still playing on the pontoon. It couldn't have been the spirit water that dragged me under, Lizzie thinks. Else how come they're all okay? They're all there, except ...

'Jimmy!' Lizzie jumps up. 'Where's Jimmy?' The other kids look at her, stunned. 'Did you see Jimmy?'

They look at each other, shake their heads.

'He's drowned,' she yells, and races round to the other side of the billabong. Can't remember seeing him, she thinks. He was there when we came, but he wasn't there when we were playing on the pontoon. What if the spirit water got him as soon as he jumped in and we didn't notice? He could have been dead for ages. That was probably his face! *No, please*, she begs.

'Jimmy! Where's Jimmy!' she screams to Mum and Dad.

And he stands up.

Jimmy.

Not even wet!

He was just sitting there with Caroleena all the time. Lizzie stops, stunned.

'What's wrong?' Dad asks her, his face worried.

Mum stands up and starts walking towards Lizzie. She wants to hold her and find out what's the matter.

'Nothing!' Lizzie says, and walks down to the pontoon, embarrassed. The little kids are still playing, jumping off and swimming back, their skin wet and shining, smiles big and white across their faces. She stands and watches them. How would you know if one did go missing? There's so many. And then, as if brought on by her thoughts, the clouds start to build up, coming together in tall masses of whiteness. Their undersides darken, grow heavy with water. The wind whips ripples across the surface of the billabong, making the little kids shiver. They stay underwater or lie on the hot forty-four-gallon drums to try and get warm. But the storm comes closer and closer.

'Big storm coming,' Dad yells. 'Come on you mob.'

They pack up camp and drive home, a wall of wind and rain just behind them.

15

The Flood

And now it really rains, all week, heavy wild rain, falling in an endless stream. Everything's covered with moisture: clothes are damp, the floor slippery with condensation, the cushions covered with a film of mould. Opium River bridge is washed away. Long Hole river's right up across the causeway. The old ladies have seen signs of crocodiles at the billabong so the kids can't play on the pontoon. It's too cold anyway to go swimming.

The kids sit in the boys' bedroom huddled around Jimmy's radio, listening to music crackle from the tiny speaker. They're sick of being wet. Usually in the Wet season it's hot and muggy all day, then it rains, cool and windy, in the afternoon. It's the best fun. But now it just rains and rains all the time. Non stop. Everything's wet. The tracks are all boggy and the lawn is black and sloshy, mud coming up through the grass. Leeches loop along the trees and shrubs, ready to latch onto your skin and suck your blood.

'Did you boys get wood for Mavis?' Mum asks.

'Yeah,' they all reply, keeping their heads down.

'How much?'

Dale holds his hand to show a pile about a metre high.

'Did you put it in the house?'

'Yeah.'

'Good boys.'

Meg and Jeweleen are sitting up at the table, looking through a book.

'You, Reuben and Tomias should stay up here tonight, Jeweleen,' Mum says. 'There'll be too many people at home.'

'Yes,' Jeweleen says, smiling at Meg.

'You two girls put your garbags on and take this down to Mavis while the rain's stopped,' Mum says, putting a basket on the table. 'Careful, it's hot.'

There's a heap of dogs under Mavis's veranda, wet and smelly. 'Get out!' someone yells, throwing a stick at them. They slip away, but as soon as his back is turned they sneak back, shaking mud and water off their coats onto the walls and floor.

There's a fire in a forty-four-gallon drum and lots of old people standing around it, huddled under blankets, holding their hands out to its warmth as if they're praying. No one looks at Meg as she comes in. There's mud at the door and muddy water flows past the veranda. Inside, the room is smoky and hot. The usual place for the cooking fire, a dirt fireplace outside, is under water, so Mavis has the fire inside. The shutters are closed to keep out the rain, and the walls and roof are black with fire smoke.

Reuben's up on the roof.

'What ya doing?' Meg asks.

Reuben doesn't really want to talk to her but she asks again, so he has to say, 'To let that smoke out.'

'But that wind might rip that tin off.'

'S'all right – just loosening it a bit.'

'You good boy Reuben,' Mavis says. 'Where's Tomias?'

'Playing cards at home,' Meg says, and then, feeling guilty that Tomias might get into trouble, she adds, 'Him and Dale were going to help Dad at the workshop.'

There's one old man sitting in the corner singing softly, his eyes closed, his body swaying. 'Is he sick, Mavis?' Meg asks. 'That old man, is he sick?'

'Mightbe.'

Mavis is normally full of information, explaining everything that happens. Now she talks real short, as if she doesn't want Meg to know what's going on.

The rain's really settled in and everyone is angry, blaming Mavis. Even her family is angry. They reckon it's her fault for taking Dale mob to Barrumbi, for not teaching them properly.

A sprinkle of raindrops fallen from the trees hits the roof, and a cool breeze comes through the wire door. Then it starts raining hard again. The water spreads up onto the veranda, around people's feet. Mavis takes the broom and swishes it out of the doorway.

'We should dig a drain to make that water go round,' Meg says, and she and Jeweleen race up to the workshop to get a shovel.

'Dad, the water's coming up on Mavis's veranda. Can we get a shovel and dig a drain?'

'Make sure you bring it back.'

Meg and Jeweleen dig and dig, making a channel around the veranda, sweating underneath their garbage bags. No one helps. The old ladies whisper to each other, 'That's what happens. The brother does that bad thing and the sister and the mother will suffer. Whatever man does will cause work for women.'

The drain is finished and fills quickly, taking the water away from the house.

'Good girl. Good girl,' Mavis says, pulling the boiling billy off the fire. The smoke makes her eyes water. She throws in a handful of tea leaves and puts the billy back on to boil again. Meg and Jeweleen grab a pannikin each, put plenty of sugar in and pour themselves tea.

The smoky room is full of people, all Mavis's relatives sitting quiet, wet and worried. None of them look at Meg. They all turn away when she comes in. There's wood stacked in the corner but it's all still wet.

Mavis hands the tea around. All the old people sip straight from the billy, warming their hands against its side, blowing softly to cool the tea closest to the edge, and breathing in the warmth as it rises steaming into the cold air.

'Mum reckons more rain coming,' Meg says.

'Big rain coming,' the old man says, looking hard at Meg. Everyone murmurs in agreement.

'Can Jeweleen, Reuben and Tomias camp up at our house, Mavis? Mum says it's all right,' Meg says.

Mavis nods. 'You mob stay up there.' She is happy to have them away from the anger in the camp. 'Reuben?' she sings out. 'Go camp na Dale's place.'

Reuben shakes his head.

Mavis goes out to talk to him quietly, her hand on his shoulder.

He walks up to the workshop.

Everyone knows that Sean's up in the escarpment. Now the big rain has come back, it looks like he did do something wrong and they're in for a big flood. They ignore Mavis, thinking she is stupid because she didn't bring him up properly. Everyone knows something really bad is going to happen. They want to yell at Caroleena, 'You shouldn't take those white people there!' But they know that Caroleena will scream at them and chase them with a stick, so they just whisper to themselves and stay in their houses, silent with resentment.

Meg feels the resentment. Mavis's house is meant to be her house. Mavis is her mother's sister, Meg's auntie or mother. They shouldn't be angry to me in Mavis's house, even if they are old people, she thinks. 'Why that mob here anyway?' she asks Jeweleen, gammon she doesn't care what they think.

'Too much water,' Jeweleen tells her. 'Bottom camp all flooded.'

'True?'

Jeweleen nods.

'We gotta tell Dad!' Meg says.

Jeweleen turns away to say the old people don't want help from Sean's family, but Meg isn't listening. 'Oh, poor old things,' she says, and as soon as there's a break in the rain she runs to the workshop to tell Dad.

Lots of people are working there.

Sandy's filling all the forty-four-gallon drums and water tanks with clean water. Dad's putting the boat motor in a forty-four full of water to make sure it's working. He fills the fuel tank and puts it in the back of the Toyoda. The boat is on the roof rack already. Rex is sealing the Toyoda distributors with a ring of grease around the lip.

'What's going on, Dad?' Meg asks.

'Just getting everything ready in case there's a flood.'

'But there's already a flood at bottom camp.'

'What?'

'All them old people from bottom camp are getting flooded. There's heaps of them on Mavis's veranda.'

'Bloody hell!' Dad says. 'Why didn't you mob tell me!' He turns to Sandy and Rex. 'You could have taken the Toyodas and picked them up.'

Sandy doesn't even look up. He's sick of trying to mediate between Sean's family and the rest of the community. Everyone blames him. He's not listening any more. Too much humbug.

'Jeweleen and Megan,' Dad calls. 'Go home and tell Mum to get the school ready! Dale! Tomias! Reuben! Go with Sandy to get the old people from bottom camp while this rain holds off.'

'How come?'

'Just go!' Dad answers, his eyes sparkling with anger.

Reuben, Dale and Tomias jump in the back of the Toyoda.

Dale hasn't seen Reuben for a couple of weeks. He knows he's ignoring him so he wants to say something smart. But Reuben keeps his head down so Dale can't even look at him smart.

'Finish that spearhead?' Tomias asks.

Reuben nods.

'You got wood for spear?'

'Rex gonna take me after.'

After. When it stops flooding. When all this trouble is over. If nothing really bad happens.

Silence.

'Sandy mob are not ignoring that old man father for Dale,' Tomias says in language. 'Us mob are still family for them.'

'Mavis said I got to go sleep their place.' Reuben continues the conversation in language.

Tomias smiles. He's been a bit worried about hanging around with Dale mob. Even though no one has said anything to him, he feels he might be a traitor or something. But if Mavis has said Reuben has to come too, then it must be all right. 'Reuben's coming to camp with us mob,' he tells Dale.

Dale's a bit confused. Tomias doesn't like Reuben, so why's he happy? He shrugs his shoulders to Tomias to say, I don't care.

The track down to bottom camp isn't used much by cars. The old people live there. People who don't like to live at the community. Who don't like whitefella food – they only like bushtucker. The only time a car goes to bottom camp is to pick up a sick or dead person or to take meat to the Traditional Owners.

The road is full of deep puddles. Red muddy water splashes up over the Toyoda's windscreen and the windscreen wipers spread it in wide arcs.

They're only half way down the road when they meet a line of old people walking. Some of them carry rifles. These men were stockmen and, still proud of that tradition, wear jeans, checked shirts, riding boots and wide-brimmed hats. A couple of the old men are too proud to wear clothes. They carry spears over their shoulders, their hair is pulled back in headbands, ripples of ceremony scars run across their bare chests like ribs. They walk straight past the Toyoda as if it's invisible. They're heading out through the community to their traditional places in the safety of the hills.

'Pick up meat at that workshop,' Sandy tells them.

One old man points with his lips to Dale in the back of the Toyoda. 'Is that young boy brother for that criminal?' he asks Sandy in language.

Sandy nods. 'He calls me uncle,' he says, but he doesn't meet the old man's eyes.

Many of the old people are tired and sick, so they stop to get a lift. They climb into the back of the Toyoda, as many as can fit. The boys get out to collect swags and the other things the old people carry. They throw them up on the roof-rack.

One old lady has a skinny dog shivering beside her. She tries to lift it into the back. 'You can't take that dog,' someone says. She ignores him, lifting and pushing. The dog is yelping in pain, her teats caught against the tailgate. The old lady's skinny arms are shaking with the effort.

Tomias and Reuben grab the dog and lift her into the back. The old lady climbs in beside her. Holding the dog's face between her hands, she tells her, 'No good. No good. Too much water,' and then says to Tomias, 'Poor fella, him crying, crying, for him baby.' There are tears in her eyes. The dog's teats are engorged with milk. She's trembling, her eyes clouded over in pain.

She must have milk fever, poor old thing, Dale thinks, and he reaches out to feel if she's hot. She growls, uncertain about his white face and different smell.

It takes two more trips to get all the old people and take them to the school. Dad follows on the next trip with the other Toyoda. He stops beside an old man and his family walking down the road. The old man throws his bedroll in the back, and tells Dad in language to drop it at Mavis's house.

'Too many people, Forty Mile,' Dad tells him. 'You can stop that workshop, Sandy's workshop.'

Forty Mile nods his head and walks on.

His wife, weak and thin, stands and waits, her head high, her back straight. Dale and Tomias jump out, let down the tailgate of the Toyoda and help her into the back. She is so skinny; even Dale's small hands go right round her arms. She's like a bird skeleton, he thinks. The old lady nods thank you, pulls her skirt around her legs, settles her bag into her lap and looks out into the country, ignoring everyone.

16
Finding Treasure

They drop the old people at the school and head back to get their possessions from bottom camp. It starts to rain again. The road is boggy and slippery. Coming over the rise, they see through the Toyoda's muddy windscreen that the billabong has gone. The floodplain that surrounds it is a mass of milky tea, not running or flowing, just slowly spreading farther and farther out. The water reflects nothing, not even the sky itself; no colour, just dark patches where ripples whipped up by gusts of wind form patterns across the surface.

They park the Toyoda as close as possible and wade in to check the houses. A pannikin floats away, bobbing on the flood's surface. Water is lapping under the mattresses on the beds. They carry them out and pile them on the roof-rack. Dale and Tomias tie the cupboards closed with baling twine through the handles so the stuff inside doesn't float away.

It's so quiet. Weird. Not roaring like the creek or the river. There's no sound except for a heavy *gulp, gulp, gulp* of air escaping as the water settles into cupboards, upturning cups and plates, lifting and moving everything around.

Dale, Tomias and Reuben go from house to house picking up anything that can be used at the school:

billycans, mattresses, big pots. They grab beds and chairs from outside, take them inside, and bolt doors and windows to keep them there.

In one of the houses there's a bundle of spears against the wall, beautiful spears, straight as straight, the wooden tips smooth and sharp.

Dale carries them outside. 'We should take those,' he says.

Tomias shakes his head.

Reuben comes up. 'Look!' he says, pointing to a dark stain on one of the spears. 'Blood.'

'Better take them, they'll get washed away!' Dale says.

Tomias and Reuben lock the shutters, grab the mattresses and walk out. They don't want to know about the spears. Dale finds some tie wire and ties them to the inside of the roof.

Dad comes in. 'What you doing?'

'Just these old spears. So they don't get washed away.'

'Don't waste your time. If he wanted them he would've taken them with him.'

'But this is Old Copper's house, and he's still up there with the other old men and Sean.'

'Dale, we haven't got room to take everything.'

Dale looks around. He sees an old tin trunk under the bed. 'What about this?'

'That'll be right where it is,' Dad says, and walks out. 'Come on.'

But Dale can't go without just peeking inside. He tries to lift the latch but it's caught. He looks around for something, a screwdriver, something to lever it with.

There's nothing. He sits down on the lid, pulls the latch, and it opens. Inside there are medals and photos. Medals like from the war. Blue ribbons with red stripes and tarnished bronze medals with pictures on them. In one photo a young black man in uniform stands straight and tall, hat on the side of his head, no shoes, holding spears against his leg.

Someone's coming. Dale turns around quickly, thinking it's Dad, but it's Sandy.

'Sandy! Sandy!' Dale says. 'Look! From the war. We gotta take this box. If they get wet they're buggered.'

Sandy looks. 'Hey. What-you-mean? Whatkind?' he murmurs.

'We gotta take it,' Dale says. 'Or they'll get wet.'

Close it up, Sandy motions with his hand. Put it in that Toyoda.

The trunk is heavy. It takes the three boys to lift it into the back of Sandy's Toyoda.

'Old Copper must've been in the war,' Dale says. 'There's photos in there with a uniform.'

Tomias and Reuben say nothing. They shudder at the sound of Old Copper's name.

'They're not dead, you know!' Dale says, suddenly angry. 'You can still talk about them. They're not dead. Sean's not dead. They're just stuck out there for the Wet! That's all!'

Tomias and Reuben ignore him.

Dale moves away from them. Bloody idiots. Old Copper, hey? Hard to believe. Didn't even know Aboriginal people got into the war. You never see them in the pictures. Fancy Old Copper fighting in the war.

He's so skinny and old, his thin grey hair piled up at the back of his head. In the truck on the way to Barrumbi, all the old men and Sean were sitting behind the driver's seat, Old Copper glaring, his blind blue eye looking about by itself from one person to another. If you're looking at him when his blue eye looks at you it will make you sick! So no one's ever game to look at him. Perhaps he lost his eye in the war! Perhaps he used it to make the enemy sick!

Dale covers the trunk with a mattress just in case Dad sees it, and they all run back to look for more stuff. But they don't find anything else interesting and Dale's glad when Dad calls, 'That'll do. Let's go.'

On his way to the car Dale walks past one tiny little house, old as anything. He nearly goes straight past, but just then the sky lightens. A sunbeam finds a hole in the clouds and makes a circle of light under the house. He stops and looks. And in that patch of sunlight there's a litter of puppies, moving, snuggling, trying to get warm. Their eyes are still sealed shut, their little voices hesitant and frightened.

Dale kneels down. Dad won't let me take them, he thinks. No way. He reckons there's too many dogs in the camp. But I can't just leave them here to drown, to be gobbled by a croc or something. 'Tomias! Tomias!' he yells.

Tomias and Reuben come round the corner. 'Look, Reuben!'

The three boys kneel down. 'Stick them in ya shirt,' Tomias says, tucking his shirt into his pants, grabbing a couple of puppies and putting them in through the neck hole. Dale and Reuben do the same and they walk away from the house with arms free, the puppies' tiny bodies struggling to find tightness and warmth, their wet noses cold on the boys' bellies.

As soon as they get back to the school, they race in to the old lady with the dog. When they hand her the puppies her face breaks into a thousand fine wrinkles, crackling with laughter. 'Ahnan,' she cries, holding them up to her face, calling the dog over and showing her. The boys leave quickly, not wanting to be caught anywhere near the dog or the puppies.

'What about the trunk?' Dale says to Tomias. They run back to the Toyoda and jump in the back.

'It's gone.'

They turn to ask Sandy but his face is empty.

They look at each other. We'll find it later, their eyes say, and they go back to carting stuff into the school.

Jimmy's sitting on the floor, not even helping, playing with his stupid radio.

'Jimmy? Take some tea over to those old men,' Mum says. Dale and Tomias smile at each other, Good job, and run out the door before she sees them. Jimmy tucks the little radio into his jeans. It's still on, the static leaches out of his pocket. 'Got a station, Mum,' he says, his face real proud. 'It's a static station,' and he laughs at his own joke.

What's that? one old man asks with his eyebrows as Jimmy hands him a cup of tea.

'What?' Jimmy says, shrugging his shoulders.

'That zzzzitt one noise.'

'Radio.' Jimmy sits down to show him. 'I'm going to get a short wave radio for Christmas. Not that Christmas. The real one, when Mum and Dad go to town.'

The old man holds the little radio in his hand. 'Hey. Too little,' he says. 'Forty Mile!' he sings out. Speaking in language, he tells him to come and look at this one radio. Little one.

'Whatkind,' old Forty Mile says, looking up at Jimmy. 'Where you find this one?'

'Na shop, town,' Jimmy says, showing them how to turn the dials and find the station. The static gets louder and softer. The old men laugh.

'Remember that one,' Forty Mile says in language. And they smile at each other, remembering the war. That was fun. Walking everywhere, chasing that Japanese plane. Looking out for army plane, Japanese plane.

'This one too small. War time. Remember. It was too big. Heavy. Too heavy,' the other old man says in language, and then, 'Sixty pounds,' in English.

'Sixty pounds?' Jimmy says.

'Big one. War time. Me and Forty Mile now carry that radio everywhere.'

'Wow, was you in the war?'

'All us mob,' Forty Mile says, showing all the old men with a curve of his arm.

'Cool. Did you have radios?'

'Biggest one.' Forty Mile shows Jimmy the size of a big box. 'Sixty pounds.' Then he laughs and talks in language with the other old men. They laugh too, remembering that time they had to go with that cheeky one officer. How they tricked him good. He was real cheeky that man. Wouldn't listen. We told him go this way easier but he follow that thing, little clock. Straight through swamp, everything.

But that one time that cheeky officer told Forty Mile to take that aerial up the tree while he played with the dials trying to get in contact with the other mob. He reckon they was lost. 'Lost? How can we be lost in our own country?' Forty Mile says, waving his skinny old arms. 'But he didn't believe, that bloke. He always want to check everything.

'Us mob pulled that wire, that antenna wire, from the radio. It couldn't hear nothing. That man got real wild. "Why won't this bloody thing work! Higher. Higher," he was telling me up the tree. Then he reckon, "Give me go," and he got up the tree hisself, skinny one, white legs sticking out from that baggy short. So funny. But he can't make it work. That wire was undone.' Forty Mile laughs and laughs, the ceremony scars along his belly and across his chest ripple; his eyes, yellow and tired with age, sparkle. 'He never like to go bush no more that bloke,' he says. 'He was frighten. He reckon we lost. Us mob,' he says, hitting his chest, still angry and offended after all these years.

Caroleena's walking along the road, her large body swaying with each step. She's worried. Her small house is full with relatives escaping from the flood. She's walking so she can think. Everyone in the community blames her for taking Sean up to Barrumbi. If she hadn't taken him then he couldn't have caused the flood. Someone is going to die now, they say.

But the worst thing is her family. They're fighting with everyone, yelling at them, sticking up for Caroleena. There will be a big fight soon. Perhaps someone will get hurt. Then the neighbours will get real wild. They might sing her or something.

As she passes the school the sun comes out, shining bright on that big white wall at the back of the assembly area. She can see the words that were embossed into its surface in old-fashioned writing, many years ago. Caroleena looks at the writing. One time she knew what it meant but she hasn't read or written in English since she was a child, when she was in the mission school. She can't remember the writing signs.

Two crows land on a little ledge. *Crawk! Crawk!* they yell, jet black against the painful whiteness of the wall. Caroleena stands still, hands behind her back. The crows walk up and down the ledge, crawking. They stop, come together and feed each other imaginary food from their beaks.

Caroleena closes her eyes. It's certain, then. If things go on as they are, someone will die. She goes straight home, picks up her dilly bag, her digging stick, her basket weaving and her swag, and she goes up to the school to make her camp with the old people.

As she walks past Mavis's house she turns her head away from the angry stares. Mavis is inside, making stew on the fire; the room is stuffy with smoke. Mavis looks out and sees her good friend Caroleena walking past, having to turn her head away. She gets wild. Without saying a word to her relatives, she picks up little Alfred and her dilly bag and walks out of the house, following Caroleena up to the school, leaving all the angry people behind to look after themselves.

The Toyodas are empty now, and Dad drives his car up beside Sandy's so they can talk through the windows.

'We'll have to take the truck over the river now before it gets too high,' Dad says. He always leaves the truck over the other side, flood time, so if someone gets deadly sick he can swim across the river and drive them to town.

'Put that tractor on. He can come back through deep water,' Sandy says.

The boys are in the back of Dad's Toyoda. This is so shaggy. A real flood! In all their lives they have only heard about big floods. The adults talk about them with such respect. They give them dates for names as if they're a war or something. The 1957 flood. The 1900 flood. It's really exciting.

If Dad notices them in the back, he'll send them to help Mum and the girls in the school, so Dale and Tomias stay quiet. When they get back to the workshop they sneak out of the Toyoda, race off home to get their bush bikes, and ride flat out down to the river crossing. Reuben and Lizzie are already there, throwing sticks into the water and watching them float down to the sucking hole.

The water's flowing over the concrete causeway in a milky mass. The edges are slow but towards the centre the water is deeper and the current strong. Underneath the causeway the water rushes through huge pipes, and now that they're covered with water the pipes suck air into them, making a spinning vortex. The sucking hole, the kids call it. It only happens when the river's really high and the causeway goes under.

When they were little Dad took them down to the sucking hole. 'You stay away from here, you kids,' he told them. 'If you fall in, the water'll grab you and hold you under against the pipes and you'll drown. We won't be able to get you out. The current's too strong. We'll have to wait for weeks till the river falls. You'd be there rotting with the yabbies eating your eyeballs. There'd be nothing left of you but bones by the time we got you out.' Then, to show them how dangerous it was, he threw a stick near the sucking hole, and *gulp!* it was gone; sucked under. He threw another stick farther away and it circled around the sucking hole, slowly at first, then getting faster and faster, till *gulp!* down it went. Even when he threw a stick near the edge of the river, it floated slowly out to the middle and swirled around the edges of the sucking hole until it got caught in the vortex and *gulp!* disappeared.

Meg and Jeweleen are washing dishes in the school canteen. Boring. This is so boring. They finish the pile Mum has left for them and – they're alone! Mum and the other women must be in the classrooms with the old people.

They look at each other. Let's get out of here, Jeweleen says with a twist of her head, pointing her lips towards the door.

They fold the tea towels neatly on the bench and slip out.

'Come past the office so they can't see us through the windows,' Meg says, and they run around the building and through the gate and onto the road. Now they don't know what to do, where to go. Can't go home. That's the first place Mum will look when she's got another job for them to do.

They see a movement down the end of the road. It's the truck, heading down to the river with the tractor on the back. 'They're taking the truck across the river!' Jeweleen says, and they both run down towards the causeway as fast as they can go, jumping over puddles, trying to keep their shoes clean. But the whole road is muddy, so half way down they have to stop and take their shoes off, hang them up in some shrubs on the side of the road. Then they can run properly, fast, holding their skirts up high and going straight through the puddles, the muddy water splashing up their legs.

17

The Sucking Hole

Dale, Tomias, Lizzie and Reuben hear the truck and duck into the bush to hide. Dad doesn't like them hanging around the causeway near the sucking hole. If he saw them, he'd send them home.

The truck comes down the bank, brakes squealing. It moves into the river and onto the causeway, and the bull-bar pushes the water up before it in a wake. The wake fans out on either side in a V.

Dale steps onto the causeway and starts to walk behind the truck.

The water in the river murmurs. It remembers Dale's warmth. It wraps itself around his feet, slipping under his toenails, into the cracks of his heels, softening the scabs on his cuts, moving into his bloodstream, tingling in the redness quickened by his speeding heart. *Come on, come on*, it says. *Come with me.*

Dale walks along the causeway, his mind blank.

What are you doing? Tomias wants to ask. But Reuben's stepping forward too, so he follows.

The boys walk right behind the truck. They stay close to the tailgate so Dad can't see them in the mirrors. The water is half way up their shins and the current's strong. They don't tease each other or dare. There's no 'Bet ya too scared to go near that sucking hole' or anything like that. It's just like, once they're walking, once they're on the causeway with the water wrapping around their legs, they can't hear anything else but the *slurp, slurp* of the sucking hole. They're not even talking to each other.

'Meg, what are they doing?' Lizzie says. 'Hey, what ya doing? What are youse mob doing?' she yells loudly.

But they hear nothing, just the *gulp, gulp, slurp, slurp*. The rippling swirls that curl around the noise draw them in closer and closer.

'It's the water, Meg, the spirit water! It got Dale at Chinaman Creek. It nearly drowned Jimmy. That's what pulled me under at the billabong. It's making them go out. That's what it does. *Stop! Don't go! It's the water!*' she screams.

Reuben stops. He sees something through the water and bends over to pick it up. A coin? 'Check this out,' he says to the other boys, but they don't hear him. He tries to prise it out but it's stuck. He looks up. Dale and Tomias are right out in the middle of the causeway. Then he hears Lizzie yelling, 'Reuben, come back! Tell them to come back!' and he turns and walks quickly back to the bank.

Once Reuben's gone, it seems that Dale and Tomias are silently competing, daring each other to walk closer and closer to the sucking hole. Reuben stopped because he's a scaredy cat. Neither of them wants to be a scaredy cat. Dale does want to stop; he can feel the water calling him, the coldness, the same caress he felt on the tube and in the water at Chinaman Creek. Why doesn't Tomias stop? he thinks. Please make him stop. But

Tomias can't stop either. The water wraps around his legs, its warmth seducing him, guiding him down into the swirling hole.

'What do you mean, the spirit water?' Meg asks.

Lizzie runs towards the causeway, shouting, 'Dale! Tomias! Don't! Don't!' But as soon as her foot touches the water it's like electricity zapping through her legs. She runs back to the shore. '*Megan, do something, they're going to die!*' she screams, and she bolts up to the workshop to get Sandy.

On the causeway the truck's wake washes over the sucking hole, covering it like a blanket. The loud gulp, gulping stops for a moment and the water is flat. The spell is broken. The boys look up. The truck comes out the other side, water running off its back. The engine roars and it climbs up the steep bank to high ground.

Dad has to take the tractor off the truck before he can drive it back. That'll take a while. Long enough, Dale and Tomias reckon, for them to watch the sucking hole start up again. They look at the flat water and watch as it slowly starts to spin around, round in a spiral, round and round, drawing everything in.

'*Get out of there, Dale!*' Meg yells. '*Dale, get away, you'll get sucked in!*'

The boys look up. Reuben, Meg and Jeweleen are standing on the bank. Scaredy cats. It isn't so scary, this sucking hole. It's not scary at all. Look, it's right there, sucking away. It can't drag us off the causeway or anything. We're safe as long as we're not in the water.

Dale looks up at Tomias. Tomias is leaning, his eyes looking, looking. 'Ahhh!' Dale yells, and he grabs Tomias, pretending to push him in. Tomias screams and jumps back. Then he laughs and gammon tries to push Dale in. Dale ducks under his arm.

Meg panics and runs towards them through the water, screaming, '*Don't be stupid, Dale, you'll die!*'

They laugh, pushing and shoving each other, and then, when she gets close, they run around her and back towards the shore.

Meg stands still. The water's making ripples around her legs. The sucking hole is just there, a couple of metres away. It's like a dark spiral, slipping round and round like a plughole or a cyclone. The water wraps around her legs, silky, warm and smooth.

Suddenly hands grab her, push her towards the water, holding her at the same time.

'Yukki!' she screams.

The boys laugh, delighted.

She spins around. 'You bloody idiots!' She swings her arm to hit them, and slips. Her leg scrapes against the rocks. She pulls back and starts to slide into the water. Falling, she tries to steady herself, waving her arms.

The boys are running away, looking over their shoulders, laughing at her flapping arms. She slips farther in; the water wraps around her waist, holding.

They stop – 'Meg!' – and run back. 'Get out of there! Hang on!' Their eyes are wide with fright.

The water pulls Meg away from the causeway and into the river.

'Meg! Swim! Dale, get a stick!' Tomias shouts.

Dale's too shocked to move.

Tomias leaves him and runs towards the bank, grabs a bamboo pole caught on the edge and runs back to Meg.

Meg's swimming hard against the current and staying steady. But she's not getting any closer to the causeway. Tomias holds the bamboo pole out to her. Can't reach – he goes down closer, Dale holding onto his shirt so he doesn't fall in. 'Get the bamboo!' they yell.

Meg looks up and swims faster, looking at the bamboo pole and stretching out her arms. She nearly touches it. Reaching, reaching. She tries to grab the pole but she has to stop swimming while she reaches out, and the water takes hold, surrounds her, sucks her under. The milky water flattens over her head.

She's gone!

'No, Meg!' Dale screams. 'It was just a joke!'

The water slips under Meg's clothes, spins around her legs, lies on top of her, drawing her down into the darkness. *Yes*, it murmurs. *Now.* It's become so much stronger. The sheer mass of itself, the speed of its current, feel good. Solid, strong and invincible, it rips dirt from the banks, breaks branches from trees, snatches lives and holds them.

Underneath the water Meg panics. Her wide eyes search, her arms flail about. *I'm gonna drown. I'm gonna get stuck against the pipes and die.* She sees yabbies all over her face, her eyes wide and colourless, the flesh all eaten, pink bits stuck to bone. Her brain is screaming,

No! The water's pulling and pulling her. She doesn't know what to do. She nearly screams. *No! Don't open your mouth. You're underwater. Calm down and think! Don't give in yet. Think. Think!* Everything's happening in slow motion. The water is translucent, quiet, solid. She can't see far but it's light, like milk, thin milk. She can see the lines of air bubbles getting sucked down with the current, pulling her towards the sucking hole.

Okay, she thinks, I'm going through that hole and into the pipe. There's no way I can fight it. I've got to get a big breath. If I can get a big breath and slow my breathing down, like the turtle or the holy men, it might last till I get to the other side. Gotta get a big breath. Gotta get to the surface. Go!

She kicks and swims with all her might, looking up towards the light. *You can do it. You can do it!*

And she makes it. Her face bursts up into the sunlight with a *pahhh*. She quickly looks around while she takes a deep breath right down to her guts – her mouth round, her eyes wide. The sucking hole is right beside her. The kids are screaming out, 'Megan! Megan!'

Is that Dad's voice? No way. I'm in big trouble if it's Dad. Forget it. You'll use more energy if you worry. Relax. Don't think about anything.

Her lungs are full of air.

Now, slow yourself down. Let the current take you. Make yourself as narrow as possible so you can get through the pipe easily. She points her toes, folds her feet around each other to make them one, lifts her arms up over her head, and lets go. The whirlpool spins her round and round; her body stiffens, becoming long and thin. Her mind is calm, the air moves slowly through her lungs into her bloodstream.

The water spins around her joyfully, wrapping her up like a bandage and carrying her away, murmuring, *Yes, relax, it's all right.*

Something hard scrapes along Meg's arm, ripping her skin open. The water's suddenly dark, black. I'm in the pipe, she thinks – relax, relax – and she slips through the darkness, calm, floating, floating.

And then it's light. Yes. I'm through to the other side.

She tries to push down to get her head up but her feet smash against something and are pushed hard up against her pelvis, knocking the breath out of her.

Bubbles, bright white bubbles, are tickling her face. She kicks out, pushing down, away from the rocks. Her lungs are bursting. But she can't get up. *Smash!* her head cracks against a rock, pain sears through her brain, and she can't stop it, her mouth springs open, gulping for air – sucking in the white bubbles. And everything goes black.

On the bank they see her body smash into the rocks. Dad runs down and jumps into the river, feeling about. Then they spot her farther down; her dress comes to the surface just for a moment. '*Dad, she's down there!*' Dale yells, pointing.

She's floating away. Dad swims and swims, his arms curve over the water, his boots kicking out behind, his hat floating along in the current in front of him, the kids running along the bank.

*

Under the water Meg feels her body heavy, a solid mass floating along a dark tunnel. Such peace. The water welcomes her and moves her quietly forward. Surrounding her body, holding it up. Cool fingers rub, hold, tickle. She's moving towards a light. What is it? Like a sunset, golden and red. She smiles. The world is so still and quiet. She reaches her hand out towards the light.

The water has her. It feels her stillness, the life oozing out of her. It tries to lap it up, to cling to her warmth, to suck the life from her. But it's bouncing off the rocks and into the air, breaking up, mixing with air, becoming bubbles, white bubbles, froth. It can't hold her!

The kids see her again. *'Dad! There! She's stopped!'* One minute her body is moving too fast, staying in front of Dad, then suddenly he is gaining on her. He can see her clearly. He reaches her, grabs her, turns her over. Her face, her still white face, falls back over his arm. He swings her arm around his shoulder and swims with her on his back towards the shore.

'Give us a hand!' he yells.

Sandy runs down, grabs at Meg, pulling her clothes and arms to get her out. Dad's pushing her up from the water. She is dead – floppy, soft and dead.

'Megan, Meggie,' the kids scream. 'Don't die! You can't!'

'Breathe into her – ya have ta breathe into her,' Tomias is yelling. 'She's got water – put ya mouth and breathe into her – punch her in the guts.'

Dale pulls Megan's dress over her legs.

Dad's slipping and sliding on the muddy bank. Sandy grabs his hand, digging his heels into the soft mud and pulling to help him up. Dad crawls quickly to Megan, rolls her over and pushes her hard in the stomach. Water spews out of her mouth. Then he holds her nose and breathes big rasping breaths into her mouth, over and over.

Please. Please, please make her live, the kids beg in silence.

Sandy moves back.

Meg doesn't move. She can feel the pulling and pushing. No! Leave me, she thinks. She wants to keep floating. Where's the lovely light? She searches around her eyelids. There, there, farther away. She tries to go back but it's getting fuzzy and there's this noise. She tries to focus on the light.

Who's that?

Sean? She can see Sean, his face crumpled in pain. Sean, what's the matter?

Sean looks up. 'No, Megan. No! Go back!' His eyes are full of panic.

'*Megan, don't die!*' she hears. That's Dad! What's Dad doing here? She looks quickly back for Sean again, for the lovely red and gold light and the quietness. That complete silence. Sean? He's gone. She can feel her body shaking, quivering, her heartbeat pounding.

'Megan!' Dad's crying, his sobs loud in her ear.

What's wrong with Dad? she thinks. Oh Dad! What's happened? What happened to Sean?

She tries to turn and comfort him but she's too

heavy; she can't move. She looks back guiltily. The light is disappearing. She wants to go, but Dad's crying. She has to see what's wrong first. She turns her mind to Dad's hand on her arm.

Dad breathes into Meg again and again, and then she's coughing and breathing. He pushes her over onto her side. Water dribbles out her nose. She's alive!

Big loud sobs cut through the air.

Dad's holding Meg against his knees, his shoulders jerking up and down. He's crying.

The kids look away. They've never seen Dad cry.

They move farther up the bank and sit close together with Sandy, watching. Meg stays very still. Her eyes are closed, but she's breathing.

Slowly Dad's shoulders stop shaking. He picks her up and walks past them along the road to the community, his head bare, his clothes wet and squelching. Meg's head rolls back, one arm flops against his leg.

The kids walk way behind.

In the river the hungry water screams and cries. It tries to stop, to come back against the current. It clings to Dad's hat for a moment, sucking the sweat from the band.

And then the wide mass of river drags the hungry water down over rocks and rapids, tossing it up in the air, breaking it apart, spreading it so thin that in the end it loses its hunger and lets itself float along, calm and peaceful.

And the big rain follows.

18

A Miracle

The little kids who saw Megan go down the sucking hole run crying and screaming through the community: 'That girl drown! That girl drown!'

Everyone comes out of their houses. 'What? Who?'

'That big girl for Lucy!' Then, because they can't explain in English properly, they switch to language: 'She fell into the water, got sucked under the pipes – she is drowned!'

'Who's there looking for her?'

'Old man, Dale, Tomias, all them mob.'

The people who are related to Meg cry loud wails of pain. Others stand around whispering, 'Poor thing, that girl, daughter for Lucy, brother for Dale. The flood spirit took her. It will finish now. That flood will finish, soon enough.'

Mavis's family are standing around the forty-four-gallon drum on the veranda, crying. Meg is their child, responsibility for their family. This child, they cry. This child has lost her life because she has a criminal for a brother. A brother who doesn't listen to the law. He killed his sister. He will live now. Up there, the spirit will be happy, avenged, and that boy will live.

An old lady says, 'It's always this way. Women must suffer for the mistakes of men.'

Then someone says that Meg is still alive but sleeping.

'Some people sleep before they die properly,' the old man who was singing in the corner says in language. 'It quite often takes a while to die.'

This is terrible, terrible, everyone agrees. But secretly they're relieved that it's over. It could have been worse. All those kids could have died, being stupid playing in floodwater.

Meg is alive. She just doesn't want to wake up. Mum rings the flying doctor but the airstrip is flooded so the plane can't come out. The doctor tells Mum to pinch Meg hard. She moves. That's good, he says. He tells Mum to hold her eyes open and shine a torch in them to see if they work. They do. So Meg's all right. She just wants to keep sleeping. The flying doctor tells Mum to keep her warm, and stay with her all the time. Mum and Mavis make a special bed for her in the school office.

Lizzie overhears Mum talking to Dad about brain damage; how if someone hasn't breathed for a while it affects their brain. How Meg could be stuck in a coma, asleep for years.

It's all my fault, Lizzie thinks. If I hadn't said ... The words she said are stuck clearly in her mind; she can still feel them as they poured out of her mouth. '*Megan, do something, they're going to die!*' And she sees Meg running; running out over the causeway, and her face white and terrified as the water drags her down. Please, please God, Lizzie begs. Please, if you let her not be brain-damaged, I'll stop bossing people for the rest of my life. I'll never tell anyone what to do. I'll – I'll –

Then she sees Dale. 'Megan could be brain-damaged, you know,' she says.

'What-you-mean?'

'Brain-damaged, like, you know.' She pulls a face.

Brain-damage? Dale panics. That's like … Her hands and feet will curl up 'cause she can't use them and her tongue will hang out of her head. Dale has seen brain-damage kids in town. They live at the hospital; people push them around in wheelchairs. His blood tingles. If Meg is brain-damage it's gonna be all his fault. He goes into the school office and sits by Meg's bed. *Meggie, please don't go brain-damage.* He talks to her all the time. 'Meg, you can't get sick,' he says. 'Sean's already lost and Mum and Dad would …' He doesn't know exactly what Mum and Dad would do, but it would be awful; everything would be too bad.

When Mum and Mavis come in to put medicine on Meg's scratches and grazes, Mum says, 'Dale, you're being very helpful. Thank you so much for looking after her.' And Dale realises she doesn't know that it's his fault – that he's the one what made Meg drown. And that makes him feel worse, because what's going to happen when she finds out? Tomias feels guilty too, a bit, and comes in sometimes. But he doesn't want to be in the same room with a girl, or everyone will tease him like she's his girlfriend or something.

The old people out in the assembly area don't believe Meg's alive. They saw her carried in by her father, limp and dead. They cried out, covered their mouths, screaming, wailing and keening; hitting their heads.

'Always,' they said, 'always the flood must take a life. It's a cruel world.'

Now Mavis is trying to tell them that Meg's not dead. That she's just sleeping, sick. They cover their ears, not wanting to hear that dead girl's name. They won't believe – they saw her body – she was dead.

'Come and see,' Mavis says, and she takes them in a few at a time to see Meg asleep. The old ladies put their hands on her to feel her heart beating. When they're sure she's still alive they make special signs for her and go outside to tell everyone.

That evening the sun sets behind towering white clouds, turning them pink and purple against the turquoise sky, bathing the world in golden light. The big rain is over and everything is so bright, so exactly in focus, it's as if someone has washed away the dust in the air itself. The old people cart wood out onto the oval and light fires for a corroboree. People come up from middle camp to join them. They sing about floods and death. They tell stories of pain and suffering, of their own children who have died, of people they know who have been washed away with the water.

Mum and Mavis wrap Meg in a blanket and lay her fast-asleep body on a mattress out on the oval. Lizzie sits massaging her sister's feet, thinking with all her might, trying to push thoughts into Meg's mind: *Megan, you are so brave. You are so strong. Don't die. Wake up.*

Caroleena sits by Meg's head, singing to her in language. The words float over Meg's body, tickling; they slide through her ears into her mind, caressing, soothing, stimulating; calling her. She feels the ground shaking with dancing feet and noise and hears the words; she feels Lizzie's hands pushing and pulling on her feet, but she is so tired, she just can't move.

Late at night, once all the other songs are done and most people have gone home, the old ladies gather around Meg. With Mavis and Caroleena they sing for her, special songs to keep her in this world. They do slow, shuffling dances; standing in a line and using their arms like paddles, they swim across the water to new life.

Next morning Meg wakes up.

'Meg?' Dale says as soon as her eyes open.

At first Meg doesn't know where she is, and her face is all confused, but then she sees Dale and remembers and tries to think of something really nasty to say to him. But she can't think of anything so she just glares at him.

'Are you all right? Are you brain-damage?' Dale asks.

'Piss off, Dale!' she says. She tries to hit him and hurts her scratched arm. 'Owww.'

Dale runs out. 'Mum, she's all right! She's not brain-damage!'

Mum comes in, Mavis, Lizzie, everyone running into the tiny room – *Megan, Meggie, Meg* – all touching her and laughing.

Meg's forehead crinkles up into a frown.

'Run down and tell your father,' Mum says, excited. Dale takes off, heading for the workshop, but Dad is already in the Toyoda just down the road, coming up to visit Meg.

Dale runs to the car, yelling, 'Dad! Meg's alive!

She's okay! She told me to piss off and she's grumpy with Mum!'

Dad smiles so hard his eyes nearly disappear into his wrinkles. 'S'pose they're all in there, are they?'

Dale nods.

Dad drives up to the workshop to tell everybody. Dale stands on the running board, holding tight to the roof-rack, leaning hard against the door so he doesn't fall off as they bump through puddles.

As they go along Dad wraps his arm around Dale in a tight hug, just for a moment. Then he needs both hands on the wheel again, so he lets Dale go.

When they reach the workshop everyone's there. Dale jumps off the running board and stands back listening to everyone laughing, crying and carrying on about Meg.

'That young girl been die. Old man been kissim. Put that air inside,' an old man tells everyone. 'Na?' he asks for confirmation from Dad.

Dad nods.

'She die. Then she come back live,' the old man says.

'Like that baby Jesus,' an old lady says, holding her head high, proud that here in Long Hole they've had a miracle.

That afternoon everyone in the whole community comes to see Meg. 'Aihh, poor thing,' they say, touching her leg. 'She been die.'

Meg gets tired and cranky so she closes her eyes, not opening them for anyone. Even when Caroleena comes in, she keeps her eyes closed. Caroleena comes up really close and puts her ear and then her hand above Meg's mouth to feel her breath, to see if she really is alive. Caroleena is making soft noises, humming noises, keeping very still, looking, looking at Meg's face, her hands close to Meg's nose and mouth.

Meg jumps up and gammon bites Caroleena's hand.

'Yukki!' Caroleena screams and jumps back.

Meg laughs and laughs.

'Whatkind? You mightbe killing me!' Caroleena yells, laughing, holding her heart. 'You make me short breath!' Then she puts her hand on Meg's leg. 'You nomore die young girl,' she says, smiling. She sits herself down in the chair beside Meg's bed and tells her, 'You subbie find gomrdau? Nother name gornorrong.' She starts talking to Meg in language, telling her all about what fruits are ripe at the moment and what will be ripe now all through the Wet season.

And Meg listens, and she can understand some words. Sometimes she tests one. 'That's green plum, hey?'

And the moist air of the Wet season seeps into the room, and even if Meg doesn't know the names, the air reminds her what is ready. And she lets her mind wander around the community to check the big green plum tree down by the school. He'll be ripe and fat. The bush apples will be falling red from the trees. White currants will be covering the branches in the under-storey down by the creek.

'We can get that djangeli – make that red dye,' Meg says. 'He's flowering now.'

'You subbie my girl,' Caroleena smiles. 'Good girl.'

19
The Tin Trunk

Dale's really tired. He hardly slept last night, waking up all the time, checking to see if Meg was alive; dreaming about Meg's face eaten by yabbies, a crab coming out of her mouth. Seeing her body tumbling over the rocks, limp and dead. Her face, white and lifeless; Dad sobbing and sobbing.

Round the back of the workshop there's a lean-to where Sandy sleeps if he's in trouble with his wife. Dale walks out there and climbs up on the bed. The mattress is cool and damp, soft. He closes his eyes, relaxes, and then he remembers the trunk. I bet it's here in the workshop, he thinks. He jumps up. In the office? He runs into the office to check under the desk. Under the workbench? The racks? Or round behind the wood pile? With the motors on stands in the corner? He runs from one place to another, checking. Nothing. Nothing. Nothing. It's big. It's a big trunk. It's not like they could just hide it anywhere.

He goes back to the lean-to. The bed? Under the bed? And there it is, tucked right back under the bed. Dale grabs the handles and tries to pull it out. But it won't come. Can't move it. It's caught. He has to lift the bed up to get it out. Get something to chock it up, bricks.

Higher!

Another brick on each side.

It's free. He pulls it out.

The trunk is rusty red tin with a curved lid. Inside it's dark. It smells musty and precious, like Mum's special papers box. Dale sits, his body leaning against the cold metal, his arms deep inside the box, touching. There's something wrapped in cloth at the bottom. Must be an important ceremony thing. An electric shock rushes up his arm. Waaa! Electric shock?

Then he realises that when he was leaning over the edge of the trunk it was cutting off the circulation to his arm. That will give you pins-and-needles and feel like a shock, he tells himself. But just to be safe he doesn't let his fingers go anywhere near the wrapped-up important thing again. He picks up the photos and the medals, feeling the cool bronze of the medals, the softness of the thick faded material attached to them, the smoothness of the photographs. In the trunk tiny silverfish dart from one hiding place to another. A fat bush cockroach with white stripes across its black back tries to tuck itself under the layer of debris on the bottom.

There's three medals and lots of photos. That's got to be Old Copper. It sort of looks like him, but he's fit and strong, his skin shiny and black. He's a young man in an army uniform. In one photo there are six men. It's like they're on patrol or something – bundles of spears leaning against their shoulders. Why haven't they got rifles? Wonder how they got these medals. Got to find out what they're for. One looks like a Japanese medal.

Can't take them. Dad will kill me if I take them.

Do a rubbing, like you do with coins. To get an impression on paper. Yes!

Dale runs out into the workshop to find a pencil – there's one of those thick flat workmen's pencils on the bench. Now paper! In the office he shuffles through the desk and the filing cabinet. Hurry, someone will come back soon! Some nice clean paper.

He presses the paper hard against the medals so the designs show through. Then he scribbles over them, and the designs emerge, black against a background of grey pencil.

Carefully he folds the paper and puts it in his pocket. Then he puts all the stuff back in the trunk and pushes it under the bed. Whew!

There's a noise in the workshop.

Quick! Dale climbs under the bed, next to the trunk.

Old Forty Mile comes into the lean-to. He sits on the bed mumbling and complaining. Too many women up at the school, wailing and crying, laughing and talking. Man can't think. He lights a smoke and sits back on the mattress. His weight squashes the wire springs down on Dale's head. *Clunk.* The springs catch in his hair. He quickly turns his head sideways so it doesn't get squashed and his hair is pulled out by the roots. *Owww!* he mouths. His head's pressed against the concrete floor. Forty Mile's grey cracked feet with their long turned-up toenails are right next to his eyes. Lucky his feet don't stink, Dale thinks. Oh no! I'm going to be stuck here until he goes to sleep.

'Ahh,' Forty Mile says. He finishes his smoke and lies down. *Creak!* The springs groan and moan and sink down on Dale's back, squashing his whole body onto the floor. He has to breathe really shallow. The trunk is pressed up tight against his feet so he can't stretch properly.

Brrrrp! There's a really loud noise.

Dale's eyes open wide. Oh *no*!

Then *Brrrrp!* again, even louder.

Slowly the smell sinks down – heavier, as smells are, than the air around them. It oozes down, down to Dale. He can't move. He just has to lie there in the stink, as thick as rotten egg gas, worse than a flying fox colony in the Wet season. That's what it is! The old man's been eating flying fox! That's exactly what it smells like. Dale's gut jerks upward, filling his mouth with bile. He clamps his hands over his mouth. *Stop!* he tells himself. *He's going to hear you.* With his hand tight over his mouth to keep the vomit in, he makes himself swallow. Yuck! It's horrible. *Hold your breath, don't breathe. Don't breathe.* He holds his breath till his brain starts tingling. He pulls his shirt up over his face to try and make a gas mask. He holds his nose, but still the smell seeps through.

Above him, Forty Mile groans and rolls over. *Brrrrp!* Dale's facing outward so the smell hits him straight in the nose. His gut lifts again, trying to vomit the air away. He tries to breathe shallow through his mouth, to take in the smallest amount of air possible. Closing his eyes, he tries to imagine himself down the creek, up a tree, even out on the road, anywhere but here under Forty Mile's bed suffocating in rotten flying fox farts.

It takes a long time for the smell to dissipate, but finally Dale can let his nose go and it's not so bad. Forty Mile has been still for ages. Perhaps he's asleep.

Then *Brrrrp!* again, and Dale quickly grabs his nose and mouth.

Forty Mile rolls over and the wire springs bounce up and down on Dale's head and down his back. 'Where's that box?' Forty Mile says, sitting up.

Dale's eyes nearly pop out of his head. Any minute now Forty Mile's face is going to appear under the bed and he'll be discovered. His heart is racing. Why do you do this, Dale? he asks himself. How the hell do you get into so much trouble?

Then, 'Nah, waitawhile,' Forty Mile murmurs, and lies down again.

Whew.

The minutes tick past. Outside Dale can hear little kids playing. A car drives past; someone yells, 'Where's Dale?' There's a sprinkling of rain on the roof. It's hours before Forty Mile starts to breathe deeply, as if he's asleep, and Dale dares to sneak his head out from under the bed. Yep, he's lying on his back, mouth open, breathing in loud snuffling snores. Dale can't lift his body more than a few centimetres off the concrete so he has to leopard crawl out from under the bed, but once he's free he crawls so fast he looks like a millipede, scrambling across the floor and round the door. He gulps at the fresh air, feeling it wash through his body as he jumps up and bolts out of the workshop into the sunlight.

Forty Mile turns on his side just as Dale disappears round the door frame. He opens an eye and smiles. 'That might teach that cheeky boy,' he whispers, and laughs.

*

The monsoon has gone, taking the endless rain. During the day the clouds lift themselves high in the sky, light and fluffy, and the sun beats down on the community, evaporating the moisture, making the air humid and hot. The spear grass jumps out of the ground bright green, rushing in thin spikes towards the sun. Sweat glistens on the kids' skin, making it cold as they run against the air. The whole world is green, so bright green it hurts your eyes. In the early afternoon the clouds build up black and heavy, and then at three o'clock rain pours down.

As night falls the clouds, empty now, spread like a thin blanket across the sky, trapping the heat in, pressing it down on the community. In middle camp people take their beds outside to catch each breeze. They swat mozzies in their sleep. At Dale's house everyone has a shower and climbs into bed still wet. They lie on top of their sheets sweating, waiting for the brief coolness as the fan passes over them on its circuit across the room.

Gradually the billabong slips back down the hill, leaving bottom camp covered with a thick film of grey silt. On the concrete floors there are ripples of sand, just like at the beach. Dale doesn't want to clean it up – he likes the way it looks. But Dad and Sandy come in with high-pressure hoses, sucking water from the billabong and swooshing all the wavy patterns off the floors, all the soft powdery clay off the benches and out the door. The grey mud on the ground dries up to dust and spikes of green grass break through and run everywhere to make a thick mat. The old people start moving back into their homes.

*

As soon as the creek drops Mum and Dad go to town and buy mobs of food and the Christmas presents. Dad brings home a bucket of sweet pink milk.

'What this?' Dale asks, slurping a whole cup down in one gulp.

'Strawberry milk.'

'Who makes pink milk?' Jimmy asks.

'It comes from horses,' Dad says.

'Right!' Lizzie and Dale don't believe him.

'It's true,' Jimmy says. 'You know how black-and-white cows make cow's milk, well, strawberry-roan horses make horse's milk, hey Dad?'

Dad's eyes open up wide as he tries to stop laughing. He nods.

They help Mum bring in the Christmas presents. There are so many. Piles of them. But Mum goes and puts them up in the linen cupboard.

'It's not fair,' Dale and Lizzie say. They've been waiting all day to open their presents.

Mum looks hard at them. 'I think we can wait for Sean and have a proper family Christmas together, don't you?'

They look down, embarrassed.

'And Dale, no peeking,' she says.

Dale looks up, his face shocked. He never peeks. He looks at Lizzie. She's the one. She never can help herself. She's the one who always sneaks down and peeks.

Lizzie keeps her face real innocent, her green eyes wide. She opens her hands and shrugs her shoulders to say, It's not my fault, I didn't say it was you.

Dale scowls.

But then Mum says, 'Come and eat.' And they've got all this food they haven't had for ages. They scoff fresh apples one after the other and Dad heats up a huge pile of saveloys for them to dip and double dip in tomato sauce. There's a new tin of powered milk, so they make powered milk cream – lots of milk powder with a little bit of water, so it's full of dry lumps that burst like sherbet in your mouth – so yummy.

That night Dad cooks thick pork sausages on satay sticks and they have cold Milos with the crunchy Milo powder all over the top of the milk. They go to bed, sleepy with fullness.

20
Finding Sean

Every day now the old men walk up into the hills around Long Hole and look right out to the far horizon. They're looking for signs of fire, the fires the old lawmen and Sean will light on their way home. At first the kids follow them every day, but there's never anything to see so they stop going. Then one day, 'Look, smoke!' Tomias yells, pointing up at the hills behind the billabong. 'Smoke!'

The kids stop. Is it smoke?

How come? The whole land's covered with green spear grass. It's far too green to burn!

'They singing out to them mob,' Tomias says, pointing with his chin to the Barrumbi escarpment, where Sean and the old men are.

'They must've seen something,' Dale says, and he starts running through the grass. The other kids catch up with him as he reaches the hillside. Slipping and sliding on the loose rocks, they run in a straight line up the wallaby tracks, the tall spear grass brushing against their sides.

'There, look!' Tomias says, excited. Everyone gathers around trying to look down his arm to see where he's pointing.

'Where?'

'There!'

'Gammon!' Dale says. He can't see anything.

'There, look!' Tomias says, getting impatient, pointing with his lips to the thin lines of smoke rising, hardly visible against the grey sky. He looks around for Jeweleen. Catching her eye, he lifts his eyebrows, asking if she can see the fires.

Jeweleen nods, her face breaking into a smile. 'They're coming!' she says, all excited, and runs down the hill to tell Meg. Jeweleen's in love with Sean, everyone knows that. She reckons she's going to marry him. She always covers her smile and giggles when he walks into the room.

'Ah, I can see them,' Lizzie says. 'Look, Dale, you can just see like a ... a sorta lifting or something. Like lines of lifting air?'

Dale looks and looks.

'Why so many? Why they lighting so many?' Lizzie asks Tomias.

'To show they're coming home. They walking.'

'Gotta tell Mum,' Dale says, and starts to run.

'Wait! What if Sean's not with them. What if he's ...'

'What?'

'I don't know, just ...'

Jeweleen's already gone.

Shit!

From her bedroom window Mum sees the smoke. Yes, she thinks, they've made contact. They're coming home. Better go and tell Dad. She picks up little Susan and calls Leroy.

'Just fixing,' Leroy answers from the kitchen.

'Fixing what?' She runs into the kitchen and sees that Leroy has tipped the whole new big Milo tin all over the floor.

'What are you doing?' Mum yells. This always happens. There's always so much mess. Can't get anything dry with the rain – kids walking mud into the house – now this. She wants to slap Leroy hard. But then he looks up. 'Making chocolate cake,' he says, his face open and full of trust. His blond curls just like Sean's when he was little. *My baby.* She looks at him. *In no time you'll be grown up like Sean.* 'Come on then.' She puts Susan down and sits on the floor. 'Let's make a chocolate cake. But we don't need all the Milo. Let's put some back in the tin.'

'Me lo, Me lo,' Susan says, crawling over to help.

The kids walk home slowly. What if Sean's sick or dead? They don't want to know. They don't want to see Mum and Dad's pain. It was bad enough with Meg.

He's gotta be okay, Dale thinks. He's gotta be.

Lizzie crosses her fingers and her arms and rolls her tongue over in a kind of crossing to make Sean be all right. She even tries to walk with her legs crossing over, but she nearly trips.

They walk around on top of the flat-top hills and down the rock face into the spring. The rainforest floor is wet, a soft sponge of matted roots, decomposing leaves and sticks. The little spring creek falls down over mats of roots, yellow and pink at the tips where they're sucking moisture and nutrients from the water.

They follow the wallaby tracks beside the creek. It's calm now. Still full and flowing fast, but calm. Perfect for tubes, but no one even thinks about going swimming.

When they get home they stand outside talking for a while until Tomias and Reuben say, 'Going,' and wander off under the darkening sky.

Lizzie and Dale hear the radio crackle loudly in the lounge room. 'Saltbush Floodplain to Long Hole. Saltbush Floodplain to Long Hole.'

They both cross their fingers and close their eyes.

'Long Hole,' Mum's voice answers. *Could it be? Please make it be Sean.*

'Tony here,' a man says. 'From Opium River. Just mustering the buffalo from the floodplain and found something you might be interested in.' His voice sounds light and cheerful.

There's a crackling silence for a moment.

'Mum?'

'Sean! Oh my God, Sean! Are you okay? Where are you? What ...?'

The kids run inside. Dad jumps up from the table. Everyone rushes around Mum, whispering to each other, 'Sean. It's Sean.'

Mum's silent, swallowing her voice over and over, holding the handpiece to her heart.

'All us mob hunting na floodplain. This one here been looking fire.' His language is stilted, weird.

Mum automatically goes to say, '*We*! Not *us mob*!', but she bites it off and says, 'Are you okay? Are you coming home?'

There's silence.

Tony's voice comes over again. 'Don't want to chance bringing them across the floodplain now with the light going. My luck we'll hit a big swamp dog and flip the airboat and feed the buggers for the rest of the Wet season. Bloody crocs are all over the place. Really spread out this year. Come up with the flood. Lost three buffalo already. Ripped the face and neck off one – still alive – had to shoot it this morning. I'll camp up here with these mob for the night and bring them all across tomorrow. First light. Hang on.' His voice becomes distant. 'You mob wanta go na that airboat, morning time?'

Muttering in the background.

His voice comes back, loud again. 'Yeah. I'll bring them over first light. Meet you where the road runs into the Saltbush Floodplain. Listen, can you ring the missus? Over.'

'Yes! Please. Thank you ... Over?'

'No worries! Over and out.'

Mum turns around. Her face is pink with joy, her eyes sparkling. The kids have almost forgotten what she looked like really happy. They thought she was all right until they see her now.

She rings Opium River homestead, and then claps her hands and says, 'Come on, into bed. We've got to get up early.'

'Mum, we haven't had dinner!'

'Oh,' she laughs. 'Silly me,' and then to Dad, with a worried face, 'We'll get through Chinaman Creek, won't we?'

'Yeah.'

'God, I hope he's all right. He sounds ...'

'He just sounds like someone who hasn't spoken English for a while,' Dad says. 'He's going to be fine.' Getting up, he wraps his arms around Mum, his eyes laughing at the kids over her shoulder, his face stiff as if it doesn't know whether to laugh or cry.

Mum shrugs Dad off. 'Come on you kids. Let's eat.'

She sends the kids to bed early but she and Dad stay up really late. Dale hears them talking, talking through the night. So that it feels like he's just gone to sleep when Mum comes in. 'Up you get. We're going to get Sean.'

The two Toyodas drive out of Long Hole, climbing the jump-up, their engines loud in the dark. Mum's driving one and Dad the other. The spear grass is long on either side of the road, so it looks like they're driving down a tunnel.

'You looking for cattle, Dale?' Mum says. Cattle feed on the side of the road. Headlights flying through the night sometimes spook them and they jump in front of the car in panic. You've got to keep a good watch; look for their eyes shining in the headlights. Plenty of people have been killed by cattle on these roads.

'You look good, Dale,' Leroy says. 'Don't hit that bullocky.'

'I will,' Dale says, and then laughs. 'I mean, we won't.'

Chinaman Creek's still high and Mum gammon winds her window up to stop it coming in over the top, making Dale laugh. 'It's not that high, Mum!'

Dad stops on the side of the road. Mum pulls up

beside him. The floodplain spreads out before them like oil, shining in the headlights. There's total silence for a moment while their ears forget the roar of the engine. Then the sounds of the floodplain emerge: frogs, crickets, night birds; plops and splashes from animals and fish hunting and then the *whine, whine, slap, slap* as millions of mozzies slip through every opening into the cab.

'Mum, there's heaps of mozzies.'

'Singing their blood-sucking songs,' Mum says, slapping a mozzie on her face. 'Grab the mozzie stuff out of the backpack!'

'I've already got it all over me!'

In the other car Meg and Lizzie mob are complaining so much that Dad starts the engine and backs up to higher ground to get away from the mozzies. Dale finally talks Mum into joining them. 'We'll be able to see them and drive back down to meet him. You can hear them airboats for miles.'

'*Those* airboats, Dale!'

'Those, then! Mum, the mozzies are killing me.'

'Me too,' Leroy says.

From the little rise, with a few mozzies still hanging around, they see the world become visible. First the sky lightens and separates, leaving the silhouette of hills and escarpment in dark shadow. Then a heavy white layer of mist settles on the water like a blanket, just the dark discs of red lily leaves sticking through on their long stalks. As the sky lightens the mist begins to lift, becoming loose and dense, hiding the hills. All they can see is a cloud of whiteness.

'How come there's mist? Should only have them in the Dry season.'

'It's the warm water evaporating and getting trapped under the cool air,' Mum says, but in her mind she wonders if it's the water manifesting itself in the mist, wanting to cause an accident, still wanting Sean because it didn't get Meg.

Then they hear the airboat, the *thud, thud* of its flat bottom bouncing across the water, and the screaming of the small motor spinning the huge fan at the back. Mum slams the Toyoda into gear and takes off down the hill. She jumps out of the car, leaving the headlights on so the driver can see where the road is, and climbs up on the roof. 'Pass Susan and Leroy up here to me, Dale.'

Lizzie climbs up on the roof to join Dale and Mum, but Dad and Megan mob stay in the car, windows wound right up against the mozzies.

Sitting on the roof, they're the first to see the dark shape in the white mist. 'Look!' Lizzie shows Susan, smiling. 'Look, that's your big brother Sean.'

As the patch of dark becomes larger, Mum pulls Leroy onto her lap and holds Dale's hand tight, watching the details of the airboat emerge: the large round fan at the back, the driver's long legs stretched out in front of him, the people standing beside him. There's Sean!

They jump down and run to the water's edge.

Sean steps off the airboat into shallow water. Mum rushes to grab him, but stops. For a second Jardeen's face flashes across Sean's. The same. Oh God! She has to force herself forward; to wrap her arms around this hard, thin young man's body. *What have we done to you?*

Tears flood into her eyes. She hugs him tight; his arms fall like lengths of rope from his shoulders.

No one speaks.

She holds him out to look at him. His nose is sunburnt and peeling, his shorts filthy, his legs caked with dried mud, his toenails black. His shirt sleeve torn. Thick, deliberate purple scars on his arm.

No! Why? She looks around at the old men laughing with Dad and then back at Sean, his eyes dark wells of emptiness. She turns her face away so she doesn't have to see their darkness, and holds him again. *I didn't want this to happen. Oh, Sean.* And Sean slowly wraps his arms around her, holding her tight; she can feel his heartbeat slow and steady against her cheek.

Sean looks the same to Dale and Lizzie, just a bit dirty. So they wade through the mud to get on the airboat. 'This's so shaggy! Will ya give us a spin?'

The driver, Tony, is grinning at Mum and Sean. 'Bloody mothers, hey,' he says to Dale. 'Know how to embarrass you every time.'

Old Copper and the other old man who came with Sean can't take the smiles off their faces. Their hair's sticking up all over the place, like tufts of steel wool. Dad touches their hands and they giggle with him, still feeling the exhilaration of speeding across the floodplain: the sun sparkling on the water, the whirr of the fan left behind them as they race, bouncing, bouncing across the glassy surface. Even though the mist meant that they couldn't see more than a couple of metres in front of them, they wanted to go faster.

*

The airboat takes off again to get the rest of the old men, and when they're all there and Tony has disappeared into the mist, they drive home, Sean in the front passenger seat holding little Susan, Dale and Leroy in the middle. Sean's like a rod of steel – not like a person at all.

As soon as they get home Mum runs the bath. Sean gets in and soaks for hours with lavender oil to help his burns and scars heal.

Later, when he walks into the boys' room, Dale quickly grabs his stuff off Sean's bed. 'Here, have your bed.'

'Don't worry,' Sean says, flopping onto the middle bed. He goes straight to sleep on his side.

Mum and Dad are quiet, not talking. They feel so guilty. They walk around, not touching, silently accusing each other and themselves. They can't get Sean's face out of their minds, the thick scars on his arms. His confidence crushed, gone, leaving a huge hole. Neither of them thought it would happen. Never considered that he would be so hurt, so … changed.

How could you let this happen? Mum asks herself. You knew it was a possibility. But you thought they wouldn't … You thought because he was … You thought because he was your son that it would be different – that's the truth, isn't it! she yells at herself in her mind, her face twisted with anger. You thought that his whiteness protected him. You thought you could take the best of both worlds. And it's your kids who suffer.

The poor little bastard, Dad thinks. We expect too much of these kids. It's all right for us, but this is bullshit. Why didn't Sandy tell me? He should have told me! We've been friends for years. Surely I could have ... If I had known ...

What would you have done? Dad sneers at himself. Tried to talk Sandy into helping Sean escape? You're pathetic. Sandy did what he would have done for his own son. Because for Sandy there was no other way. The most important thing is order in the world. One young man's suffering is nothing compared to what might have happened. He had no choice. If Tomias broke into a bank, what would you do? Would you cover it up and hide him from the police?

But ...!

But what? Is it any different? For Sandy there's no difference. It's only you. You and your ... No matter how much you think you respect this culture, if you really thought they were going to cut him, you would have brought him out, wouldn't you? Be honest!

Suddenly he feels trapped inside the house. 'Going to the workshop,' he says.

'That'd be right,' Mum answers, really rude, as if they've had a fight or something.

The kids look at each other. They should be happy that Sean's back, not fighting.

21

Changed Utterly

Throughout the day everyone in the house sneakily opens the door of the boys' room to check that Sean's really there, that he's breathing. He sleeps all day. Sometimes they hear a noise and stop to listen but he stays asleep, not waking up or even moving, not once.

Late in the afternoon, Mavis comes up. 'Where's that boy?' she says, her face fierce. She looks at Mum and the kids, and then she walks down the hall, her shoulders back, her head high. The kids sit down, quiet. Sean's in big trouble, big trouble. They have never seen Mavis so angry.

Sean wakes up as Mavis walks into the room. 'Sorry,' he says, sitting up and shaking his head. 'I know ...'

'You know nothing,' she tells him in language, her voice loud and shrill. 'You know nothing of the pain and suffering you put your family through. The trouble called down on this community. All for what?'

'For study,' Sean says softly.

'Study! You put an animal in a cage and you find out how an animal reacts in a cage! What good is that!' she says, still speaking in language. 'What does that tell you about the world?'

Silence.

Sean is sitting on his bed, his head down. Mavis

stands at the door, her arms crossed, her eyes dark and dangerous.

'What has gone wrong with you?' she asks quietly in language.

For ages Sean says nothing, then he shakes his head. 'It's too hard,' he says, his voice cracking.

Mavis sits on Jimmy's bed, behind Sean, so she won't see him cry and shame him. 'Learning is hard,' she says softly. 'That's what makes you strong.' But in her mind she strokes him and holds him as she did when he was little.

Tears burn behind Sean's eyes; his throat is swollen. He opens his mouth and breathes deep, right down into his belly, making his mind follow the breath, trying to disperse the fog of emotion in his brain, the ache in his throat. Mavis doesn't understand, he thinks. It's all right for her and Rex and Tomias. They have one world. But we have to live in two cultures, and it doesn't work!

And as if it's just happened, he blushes with shame, remembering his first week of work experience. How he laughed and joked with the other employees at smoko time, talking about snakes and people who are scared of snakes. Telling them about Mum. How she is so scared of snakes she can't even hunt file snake, the most docile snake in the world. How she can cook them once they are dead, but she can't walk into the water to find them, hold them while their bodies are flinging about and bite them on the head to kill them. She can chase a goanna and hit it with a stick, she can dig for yams and lilies, but she can't catch snakes. 'The old ladies reckon snake might be her totem,' Sean said, laughing.

'You a bit of a blackfella, are you, Sean?' one bloke

said. 'Totem! You believe all that blackfella rubbish, do ya?'

Everyone laughed.

Another bloke came up behind him, his arm raised. He held his hand to make a snake's head, and shoved it in Sean's face. 'Look out Sean, mightbe debil-debil snake bin get you,' he said, talking in a gammon voice.

'Maybe that's why Sean's a better snake handler than any of you,' the boss said, his face twisted with anger. 'Come on you bloody idiots, back to work.'

The workers walked out, sniggering.

'They're idiots, mate,' the boss said to Sean. 'Just ignore them. There's nothing wrong with that blackfella stuff – they know a lot more than you think.'

But Sean couldn't hear him. He felt ashamed, stupid. *Why do I believe all that stuff?*

For the rest of his work experience the other blokes teased him. 'Look out Sean, debil-debil coming. Here! Come and hold this taipan. See if Tiepin is your totem too.'

He laughed when they teased him, but inside he carried that humiliation. And over the weeks he built a wall inside himself: his family and his background on one side and himself and the rest of the world on the other. He made sure he would never say anything to shame himself again.

Now, sitting on his bed, he tries to explain to Mavis. 'In town it's different. They don't recognise …' The words are hollow in his mind. They sound stupid. He settles for, 'They don't believe.'

'But *you* know. *You* have the knowledge,' Mavis says, looking at his back.

'I know.'

Mavis shakes her head.

They sit silent for a long time.

Then Mavis gets up and touches his shoulder. 'It's done,' she says in language. 'It's over and now you are strong, you will care for your family.' The warmth of her hand spreads out into his body. They look each other in the eyes. Sean tries to smile for her and she leaves.

Mum follows Mavis outside. She wants to know if Mavis knew what was going to happen to Sean. But how can she ask? Wouldn't Rex have suffered the same fate? Or Tomias? *And what, are your children different?* Mavis could say to her.

Mavis touches Mum's hand, and when she starts to cry she holds her. She feels Mum's tears falling cold onto her back, her body silently shaking.

The kids stay inside, too scared to move. They wait for ages and ages. What the hell's happening? Sean didn't get bitten by a death adder. He's alive! But they're all carrying on. What are Mum and Mavis doing? Will Sean come out? Should they go in?

In the end Dale can't help himself—he walks down the hall, listens at the door of the boys' room and then turns the handle carefully so it doesn't make any noise. He pushes the door open just a bit to peek through. Sean's lying on his back, awake.

'You all right?' Dale asks.

'Yeah,' Sean answers. He looks tired and shaken.

Mavis give it to him proper, Dale thinks. They could hear her yelling from the lounge room.

Sean asks, 'So, what you mob been doing?'

Dale's too shocked to answer. He expected Sean to tell him to piss off. But here he is looking at Dale like he's interested. Asking him what he's been doing. Sean, bossyboots Sean, who always has to have the bed by the window, who hardly even talks to his pathetic little brothers! Sean wants to know what Dale's been doing?

At first Dale doesn't know what to say. But once he starts, and Lizzie and Jimmy sneak in to lie on Jimmy's bed and help, he tells all the stories – about hiding in the back of the Toyoda, Sir Galahad, about Sean's boot and the jess.

'We got into trouble. You should've seen Dad's face,' Dale says, shuddering, remembering.

Sean nods. 'Well, sometimes you have to trust your instincts,' he says. 'You done good.'

Dale sits up real straight and proud.

Lizzie scowls at him. She tells Sean about how she reckons the spirit water tried to drown them all. 'Really, Sean! I felt it grab me and hold me under. Jimmy too, hey Jimmy.'

Jimmy nods. 'Sort of.'

'Even Dale! Though he won't admit it. But it did get Megan,' Lizzie continues. 'It sucked her under the causeway and drowned her. She was dead. Dad had to blow air back into her.'

'Yeah, I saw her.'

'Do you remember?' Meg says, her voice so soft. No one noticed her come into the room. They look up. She's looking at Sean, her face serious. 'Did you really see me, Sean?'

'Yeah.' Sean nods.

'I thought it was a dream,' she says, looking into his eyes. 'It was so pretty and quiet. I wanted to stay there.'

The other kids are absolutely still, holding their breath, shy of listening to this conversation. It's so private. They're scared they'll get noticed and be sent away.

'But what about Dad and Mum?'

'I know.'

They look at each other for ages, as if they can read each other's thoughts.

Then, 'So what about this spirit?' Sean asks Lizzie.

And Lizzie tells him about the pontoon, and the tubes.

Dale tells him about the water at Chinaman Creek.

Sean lies back and listens to them all – not talking, just listening. They talk and talk while the sun goes down, turning the world yellow and then pink as shafts of red light shoot through gaps in the trees and bounce off the bedroom louvres. Then Mum comes in, saying, 'Time for dinner, you kids!'

They eat a big fat roast pork, Sean's favourite. It's so good to have everyone back around the table – no empty seat to make Mum sad and everyone else guilty. But the weirdest thing is the talk. Mum and Dad talk and talk about the weather, about the creek, about the old people's houses being flooded. They don't talk about Sean and what happened. And they don't say anything about Meg.

Dale nearly says, 'Wouldn't of had pig up there,' just to tease Sean a bit, knowing there are no pigs in the high escarpment. But he stops himself before it pops out of his mouth. Because in a way it's like it's a big secret that no one is allowed to talk about, like they have to pretend that it never happened at all.

When they go to bed Sean and Dale lie awake listening to the night sounds. As soon as Dale hears Jimmy's snuffling snores and knows he is fast asleep, he tells Sean about the dream. The snake dream he had at Barrumbi. And how he wanted to tell but he felt stupid.

In the middle of the night Sean wakes up – huddling alone in a small cave, his whole body aching with pain and loss: the screech of pain as the razor blade cuts through his skin. His brain thick and hurting, his eyes unfocused with tears. He sits up in bed, shaking. *It's over*, he tells himself. *It's over.* And he breathes deep into his body, calming it down, letting the breath wash the pain and anger away as if it was liquid, diluting it till it's gone and his brain is clear again.

Dale listens to Sean's breathing rasping in his throat, and when it calms down he asks, 'Did you get in the biggest mob trouble up there? Did they hurt you?'

'Nah. It's all right, mate. Don't worry. It's just …'

Silence.

'Is it really true about the dream, Dale? No bullshit?'

'Really true. Cross my heart and hope to die in a pit full of death adders, true.'

'If you have any more dreams, Dale, don't be scared to tell me.'

22
Christmas Eve Again

Next morning Mum wakes everyone up, pretending it's Christmas Eve all over again, this time for real. All the presents are wrapped up and piled in the corner of the lounge room, waiting for a new Christmas tree.

Sean comes out with his gun and puts it on the Toyoda, behind the seat. Dale and Tomias look at each other. They're going to get the roast! Yes! They rush out and jump in the back. Dad hardly ever takes them hunting. They go with Mavis mob or with Rex, but never with Dad or Sean. It would be totally beneath Sean to have Tomias and Dale come along. Then Sean comes out and says to them, 'You coming? Good.'

Dale and Tomias look at each other. Sean's so different, so ... He's acting like Rex or Sandy. Caring about teaching and helping kids. So weird. 'What if he lets us have a shot of his rifle?' Dale says, his eyes so wide and excited Tomias has to laugh.

Then Sean goes inside and calls everyone else – 'Going to get a turkey! You kids want to come?' – and Lizzie and Jimmy run out and pile into the Toyoda.

'No way! Not enough room,' Dale yells. He scowls. What's Sean's problem? He's gone all soft since going up there! You can't have little kids going hunting. No chance of getting a turn of the rifle now.

Dad jumps in to drive and they head over the causeway and turn off down the dump road. It rained last night so the puddles are full, spurting brown spray up into the air as the Toyoda drives through. They drive and drive till they get to the old paddocks where Dale's grandad planted special grass to make the cattle really fat. There are thousands of wallabies in the paddock; they breed like flies on improved pasture, Dad reckons. When the wallabies hear the car they panic and run bouncing across the road, one after the other.

The kids laugh. They're mad, them mob. Why don't they just stay there? Then suddenly one's coming straight for the car. 'Look out,' Lizzie shouts, and the wallaby jerks sideways, jumping about two metres up into the air, changing direction midstream.

'Bloody idiots,' Dad yells.

'What a sidestep,' Tomias says, laughing. 'We could use him on our footy team.'

They sit up straight then, leaning out to watch the wallabies. This is fun.

Then suddenly *whack!* something hits Tomias on the shoulder. It's a wallaby! In the back of the Toyoda! It's scrambling, trying to stand up, scratching, jerking. Its long claws scrape against Jimmy's leg. 'Ahhh!' For a second everyone's stunned, and then Tomias and Dale jump on the wallaby, Tomias holding its back legs, Dale sitting on its back.

'Dad! Dad!' Lizzie stands up and thumps on the roof of the Toyoda to tell him to stop.

He slows down. 'What?'

'Tomias and Dale got a wallaby.'

'Whatd'ya say?' He stops the car and gets out, and then he sees it. He stares, his mouth open.

'What happened?'

'He just jumped in.'

Dad shakes his head.

'Well, you got the roast,' Sean says, laughing, real proud. 'Give us it here and I'll ...'

The wallaby's still, really still. Dale lifts his hand. Its eyes are dull. It's dead!

'No way.'

'Just fainted,' Lizzie says.

Dad feels for the heartbeat in the wallaby's neck. 'It's dead all right.'

'How come?'

'Looked at Dale and died from fright,' Tomias laughs.

'Come on you mob,' Sean says. 'Give us a hand to clean it up.'

The kids rush to help. Lizzie and Jimmy run around collecting leafy branches and making a bed in the back of the car to keep the meat clean.

Tomias and Dale hold the legs while Sean skins and guts the wallaby, taking the two back legs and the tail and leaving the rest for the birds. And because Sean's so ... it's like he likes his family and cares about his little brothers, Dale's game to ask, 'How come the wallaby just died like that?'

And Sean answers, 'Wallabies have a really large amygdala. That's the panic button in your head. You know how you jump really quick when you see a snake?'

Tomias and Dale nod.

'That the one now – that's the amygdala. Wallabies

have a really big one so they can panic and get away when something tries to attack them, but if they panic too much they can have a heart attack.'

'Do we have them amegia thingies?' Dale says.

'Yeah.'

'You got a wallaby brain, Dale, that's why you always panicking,' Tomias teases him.

'Do not,' Dale yells, and then gammon panics. 'Oh no, does that mean I'm going to get a heart attack!'

'No,' Sean says, 'because humans have got a hippocampus in their brain. So when you see something that looks like a snake the amygdala makes you jump quickly so you don't get bit, and before you die of a heart attack the hippocampus says, "Nah, nah, don't worry, it's just a bit of rope" and calms you down.'

Dale looks at Tomias, wanting to say something smart to tell him, See, I haven't got a wallaby brain, but, 'Hey,' Dad says softly, and everyone freezes. They turn to look at him and he points with his lips out the other side of the car. *Turkey bustard.* Hard to see because it's standing so still. In the Dry season you can't see them, their camouflage is so good, but now, with the world bright green, you can just spot the brown feathers and the flat crewcut head.

Sean walks slowly to the car. The turkey bustard watches. Sean slides out the gun, raises it, aims. Everyone holds their breath. They can feel his finger on the trigger, pressing, pressing. And the turkey bustard ducks his head and disappears.

'One second too long,' Dad says. 'Let's go.'

'But Dad, he might stand up,' Dale says.

'Nah, it's his lucky day. Let him be.'

They drive along past the old dump and out through the open country. Turkey bustards love fruit, so there might be heaps of them looking for green plums and purple and white currants. There! A big bustard runs across the road.

'Mating season,' Tomias says.

'Yeah!'

They watch the big male bustard, his feathers all fluffed up at the front, bouncing as he runs. *Doof! Doof!*, his mating call sounds. But a big old bloke like that's too tough. They want a young one.

Dad's driving slowly. Tomias and Dale are standing up in the back, holding on to the roll cage, scanning the country.

Tomias taps the roof with his hand.

Dale looks, and just as he sees the turkey, *boom!* the rifle shot bursts the air, *crack!*

Tomias jumps out and runs over to the turkey bustard and holds it up for everyone to see.

'Yahhh!' they all yell.

'Let's go get a Christmas tree,' Dad says as soon as everyone's back in the Toyoda. They drive around the long way to Christmas Creek, a little rocky creek surrounded with cypress pines. As soon as they get out of the car the rich smell of them fills their nostrils. The ground's covered with pine needles and they have to walk with their feet curved up to stop spiky nuts sticking in their soft arches. You can see all the stumps where Dale's family has cut a Christmas tree each year for more than fifty years. New trees sprout out the side of the stumps and grow stunted and small.

The kids are running from tree to tree. 'What about this one?'

'No, this one!'

'That's too baldy round the back.'

'Here?'

'Too skinny.'

'You know, it's a waste, killing a tree just for Christmas,' Lizzie says.

They all look at her like she's myall.

'Well, look at all the stumps! This used to be a forest. We're killing it. We should take one of the regrowths.'

'They're too little!'

'No, look at this one. It's perfect,' Lizzie says. 'Anyway, even Mum says it's not good to kill trees.'

Dad and Sean look at her. 'Lizzie, you always like to complicate things,' Dad says.

Lizzie's not sure if that's a good thing or not, but when Dad takes the axe and cuts down her regrowth tree, rather than taking the top of a big one, she's happy.

23
A Real Christmas

'So Dale and Tomias are the hunters this year, providing the meat for Christmas,' Mum says, teasing them.

They blush with pride.

Mum cooks Christmas damper and a proper roast dinner. She soaks the wallaby leg in milk for a couple of hours and then rubs it all over with a mixture of olive oil, rosemary and lime juice. She fills the bush turkey with stuffing and ties its legs together with string. They go in the oven together – you can see them turning golden through the door.

The kids hang around in the kitchen smelling the food cooking and talking and listening to Mum's Christmas stories. Each year she tells them about Grandad's first Christmas at Long Hole. How when he first moved onto the land he was so poor. He had brought some cattle with him but they were breeders so he couldn't kill them. But the Aboriginal people showed him how to hunt wild animals. And every Christmas from that day to this, their family has eaten roast wallaby and bush turkey for Christmas dinner.

Jeweleen, Reuben and Tomias come to stay. Everyone eats and eats, and afterwards they sing Christmas songs and tell stories till midnight, when it's time to go to the lounge room to get their presents. All the presents are under the tree with, 'From Santa – Sorry I'm late – Got lost!' written on them.

Leroy tries to stay awake but he just can't, so he falls asleep under the Christmas tree, his arms wrapped around his presents, whispering, 'Not allowed to open.'

Little Susan climbs up onto Sean's lap and falls asleep too. Every time Mum tries to put her to bed she wakes up and cries.

The kids open their presents one at a time – everyone else watching and laughing or going, 'Excellent! Wow! That's the best!'

Every year Meg and Jeweleen want the same things: new clothes, magazines with fashion models in them, new pens and pencils and pretty paper to write on. Jeweleen opens her present and it's a new dress. She squeals and runs down to the girls' bedroom to try it on. 'Oh, it's beautiful. Meg, you should see what you've got.'

Meg feels her present. It's soft and hard. A new dress and books. She can feel Mum looking at her. She wants to be happy for Mum's sake but getting a new dress just doesn't seem so exciting this year. She lifts up the dress. It's really pretty, purple patterns all over it. 'Thank you, it's lovely,' Meg says. Then she looks at the book: *Complete Food and Medicinal Plants of Northern Australia*. 'Oh, Mum.' Meg starts to cry. 'This's so cool!' She ducks over to kiss Mum. The pretty dress falls to the floor.

'Doesn't she like her book?' Reuben asks.

'She just likes it too much,' Jimmy says, his face wrinkled into an indulgent frown.

Dale opens his present, a beautiful red-and-yellow

Vibratail. 'Wow!' he yells. He's never had his own lure before. Wicked! It's exactly the same as the one he pinched from Dad last holidays and nearly lost. He looks at Dad to see if Dad bought it on purpose to shame him. Does he know what happened? Does he know that a big croc nearly got Lizzie when she was trying to get it back? But Dad's just laughing – you can never tell with adults.

Dale's next present is a bright red handline, like Rex's. Shaggy! Then there's a book. Mum always buys him a book. Boring! But he has to open it or else she'll be sad. Oh, wait. 'Wow!' *Black Diggers*, a book about Aborigines fighting in the second world war. 'Thanks, Dad,' he says.

'Not me. Your mother picked it.'

And Mum has got her eyebrows up in that way. She knows about the trunk! Sandy must have told her, Dale thinks. He looks back down at the book, gammon flicking through it and looking at the pictures. 'This's so shaggy. Thanks, Mum.'

Tomias unwraps his present carefully. Even if he lost his last one, he doesn't want a bright red plastic handline. It will just go in his big brother Rex's box with all the other handlines and he won't be able to tell which one's his and everyone will use it. The parcel feels like a handline. He doesn't want to look disappointed. As the paper comes off he sees wood. Something wood? A wooden handline?

'It floats,' Dad says. 'It's a handline that floats. When you drop it in the water it floats.'

Tomias nods and smiles. That's shaggy.

'This is yours too,' Mum says, handing him a big box.

He takes off the wrapping and opens the box. Inside there's a smaller box wrapped in newspaper. He opens that and there's more newspaper. Everyone's laughing as he rips off more and more paper. His present gets smaller and smaller until it's about fifteen centimetres long.

Hope it's not nothing. Just a joke from Dale. Tomias's heart starts to sink.

It's a brand-new lure.

Tomias's eyes light up and he smiles so wide his cheeks hurt. This is the best!

'You can keep it in our tackle box if you want,' Dad says. 'That way the little kids can't get it.'

'Shaggy,' Tomias says, very impressed.

Now Lizzie's opening her present.

It's soft. Bet it's a dress, she thinks, disappointed. Well, she knows she needs a new dress. But … Yes, it is – it's dark pink or mauve, with dark lace around the bottom.

'A new party dress,' Mum says.

Lizzie smiles. 'Thanks.' But she leaves it on her lap. 'Who's next?' she says, trying to make it someone else's turn.

'Try it on, Lizzie,' Mum says. Everyone's looking. 'Show us.'

Lizzie lifts the dress up by the shoulders and something moves. 'Shit!' Then, remembering Mum and Dad are there, she says, 'Oh, sorry!' There's something in the dress. A mouse! It's a little soft brown mouse, looking round, all scared.

'Ahnan,' she says, and tucks him into the dress. His little face peeps out through the neckline. Lizzie's face lights up. 'Hello, little thing.'

'Do you like him?'

'Oh Dad, he's the best.'

'It's a rat!' Dale yells.

'Is not!'

'Okay. Okay,' Dad says. 'Enough,' and he looks at Jimmy to open his present. 'Jimmy?'

More than anything in the whole wide world Jimmy wants a short wave radio. His little transistor can pick up AM and FM but he wants to listen to radio from all over the world. He told Dad what he wanted but Dad said it might be too expensive. His present's a box.

Try not to hope too much, Jimmy worries. Try not to think that it definitely is a short wave radio, or it won't be.

'Come on, what are you doing?' Dad says, gammon angry. He knows Jimmy's getting his last wish in before it's too late. Jimmy closes his eyes while he pulls the paper off, and – it's a short wave radio! A really flash one in a black box. 'Wicked! Old Forty Mile will think it's excellent!' he says.

Everyone looks at him, wondering what Forty Mile has to do with anything.

'Him and Old Copper mob, they were in the war you know. They used to carry the biggest radios – sixty pounds (that's like dollars in the old days) worth of radio. They were hunting for Japanese. Those Japanese in the old days, they were the worst. They pulled people's fingernails out and everything.'

How come Jimmy knows about that? Dale thinks. About Old Copper and war and stuff? He's just a kid. What's he doing knowing about that stuff? And as if that's not bad enough –

Lizzie goes, 'Your turn, Reuben.'

And Reuben opens his present, and it's *Aborigines in the Defence of Australia*.

Not fair! Dale thinks. That book's heaps better than *Black Diggers*. It's got this coolest picture on the cover – a soldier dressed up like Rambo, looking real dangerous.

Then Mum goes, like she's real interested, 'Your grandfather's in there. Want me to show you?'

'What?' Dale is horrified. Reuben's got a grandfather in the war? No way! This is so unfair!

Lucky Reuben goes, 'No, later,' gammon all shy. 'Sean's present first.' But Dale still glares at him. How come other people get all the really good stuff?

Sean looks at the presents that are left: one short, one square. The square one looks like a microscope. All year he has been asking Mum and Dad for a microscope so he can pull animals apart and study their insides. Now he doesn't want it. He doesn't want to look at dead things, to study them dead.

You should have told them you didn't want it, he thinks. Microscopes cost so much. Now they've gone and spent all this money and ... He moves Susan off his lap and tries to look excited, opening the box slowly, making his face look pleased and ... It's a rod and reel. One that folds down, right down to only thirty centimetres long – to fit in a ... a new backpack. He puts the rod in the backpack and puts it on the floor. Tears glisten in his eyes. He lifts Susan up and cuddles her tight against his chest. 'Thanks,' he says, his voice croaky.

Dad stands up. 'Okay, everyone to bed,' he says. 'It's late, nearly one o'clock.'

'Me and Tomias are in high school,' says Dale. 'We can stay up late!'

'Not till next week you're not!' Lizzie answers.

'You older kids can stay up a bit longer. Reuben, Lizzie, Jimmy, bed!' Dad yells.

'Not fair,' Lizzie complains.

24

The End

Down at bottom camp the old people are sitting around the fire under the night sky. They have danced and watched the corroboree. They have all the stories now: Meg's death and rebirth; the flood; Sean's redemption. The moon's high in the sky and the fire glows on their skin, shiny black. The sharp clap of sticks and the drone of the didgeridoo fill the air.

The old ceremony man feels good. He hasn't done all these ceremonies for many years. 'We have got complacent,' he says in language. 'We have been complacent and now we have seen what happens to people who are complacent. Our community will be washed away with flood – the earth will be cleansed of all our lives.'

The old people talk. This is a dangerous time – we must be more careful – too many young men are going to town – they don't understand their country – they are going to school and learning only to be arrogant about tradition. They have got to learn both ways – if we don't teach them, it is a big mistake. That mistake has nearly killed us this time – nearly washed our community away. We must teach them after their first year at boarding school – before they get too indoctrinated by the scientific whiteman's attitude – we must take them away to do ceremony. It was a hard job with that young boy – it was nearly too late for him. Next Wet season, they say, next Wet season we will take Dale and Tomias before they become too hard to teach.

The music sneaks up across the green country to Dale's place.

Sean doesn't have bad dreams any more. He sleeps light, so as soon as the panic starts to lift the hairs on his skin, he wakes. He remembers the murmuring of the old men's voices telling him to hold his breath and then breathe hard and quick through the pain, quietening his panicking heart. And now the sound of the corroboree drifts up from bottom camp, slipping through the louvres, entering his mind and soothing it into deep sleep.

Lizzie's lying in bed listening too, her little mouse snuggling into her hair and tickling her ears. She's wearing her new purple party dress to bed so she doesn't have to waste time getting dressed in the morning. Tomorrow Miss Wilson's coming back. Miss Wilson. It will be so good to be at school again, learning. This year her and Reuben will be the Year Sevens. It's going to be so cool without annoying Dale. But Tomias – Lizzie's heart pumps faster when she thinks about Tomias leaving, being gone for months. Her throat gets all thick and sore. *I'm going to miss him.*

Meg lies on her bed, her arm behind her head, twisting her hair around her fingers. Through the window she can see the moon hanging silver in the black sky. Bukulurl, she thinks. The songs from bottom camp float over her, sinking into her mind. The old people are organising the world she knows and in which she feels safe. It's time now to collect those little yams on the roadsides. Have to ask Mavis if we can go tomorrow, she thinks, remembering the crunchy taste of them. What's their name? She thinks about the long yams and cheeky yams growing in the forest now. Soon the rains will stop and they will suck back all the nutrients from the leaves and put them into their roots, making large underground tubers. She smiles, thinking about the women walking and digging, laughing with each other while they dig the yams. School next week. What subjects will I have this year? Hope I can get into biology and learn heaps more about plants and animals.

Jimmy's mind is racing with information. Tomorrow he'll go down and show Forty Mile and Old Copper his new short wave radio. It's right beside his head, softly whispering to him in weird languages – it's real funny. They're going to love this, he thinks.

Tomias feels sick. Him and Dale really are going to boarding school. Just a few days and he'll be leaving the warmth of his brothers, of Mavis, to go and sleep in a line of stiff beds. What will that be like? Dale's mum reckons she'll come in and visit each week for the first semester, to make sure they're all right. But they won't be able to come home. He lies and listens to the insects whispering outside. In the distance he can hear corroboree. He moves his head to listen more carefully. Bottom camp. It's coming from bottom camp. They're singing for us, those old people.

Dale's just falling asleep when the sound of the corroboree comes into his mind. Bottom camp, he thinks. Old Copper – the medals! He can't wait to go to boarding school. They've got a huge library at the school and another one in town. You can borrow books about everything in the whole world, Sean reckons. They would definitely have books on medals and uniforms and stuff. Got to find out about those medals.

He slips his hand under his pillow to get the rubbing of the medals. And he can't find it – it's gone! He sits up quickly and pulls his pillow out. Nothing. Oh no! His pillow case is changed. Mum must've washed the sheets and pillowcases. No! He flops his head down on the pillow. No way! This is so unfair! He sits up, punching the pillow.

'Dale,' Tomias says.

Dale looks up.

Let's go, Tomias says in his mind, flicking his fingers to say he wants to go outside. And although he hasn't spoken aloud, Dale hears him and sees his fingers in the darkness.

They get up, ease the door open, tiptoe down the hall past Mum and Dad's room, and slip out the back door. It takes a minute for their eyes to adjust to the darkness. The moon is bright and high.

They run in the grey light across familiar ground to their old schoolyard. Their classroom's small and white, standing on stilts beside the big mango tree. They walk up the stairs. The classroom's always left open in case kids have trouble at home and need a place to sleep. They open the door and slip in. The light coming through the louvres shows the desks, little dark squares on the wooden floor. The large darkness of the blackboard at the far end. They sit at their desks in silence.

'We should do something,' Dale says.

'What?'

'I don't know. Rig up a bucket of water over the door. Fill a balloon with water and when Miss Wilson opens the door it'll drop all over her. No! Fill it with air. It'll go off like gunshot. Or we could put a snake in her desk.'

Tomias looks at him. 'What?'

'Not a dangerous one. One of Sean's. Arcilies or Anzac. Or … I know! C'mon, I'll show ya.' Dale runs out, and next minute Tomias can hear him climbing up the mango tree. 'We could put a greenants' nest in Miss Wilson's desk! … Owww! Get lost, you buggers.'

Tomias follows, laughing. The mango tree's full of greenants at this time of year so he climbs up the drainpipe and onto the roof. Dale jumps out of the mango tree with a thump, wiping greenants off his arms and legs, and runs up to the peak of the roof to lie down.

They're on their backs, arms behind their heads, looking up at the sky. The vast blackness of it opens out around them. The moon is huge, its yellow light melting into the sky like an aura. 'Ring around the moon – bad times coming,' Dale says, gammon real ominous. They lie still watching the clouds move past the moon, holding their shape: a ship in full sail, a huge frog, an owl with the biggest eyes. Stars really do twinkle. The planets are solid dots of light but the stars twinkle like diamonds in the thick moist air.

'See them pointers from the Southern Cross, Alpha and Beta Centauri? It takes four years for the light from them to reach Earth,' Dale says. 'Some of them stars is already blown up – it's just the light still coming down.'

A shooting star flashes across the sky.

Tomias closes his eyes.

'Make a wish,' Dale says.

Wish boarding school burns down, Tomias thinks.

'The Southern Cross is our constellation. Mum reckons no matter where we go in the world, even if we get separated, we just look at the Southern Cross and connect to each other.'

Silence.

Honk! Honk!

They turn their heads to see a great V of geese, dark against the sky, honk honking right above them.

Dale smiles, spits on his hand, and goes, 'Oh yuck, bloody goose shat on me!' Quickly he gammon wipes the wetness onto Tomias.

'Get out!' Tomias yells, rolling away. 'Bloody idiot!'

Dale kills himself laughing. 'Just spit. Got ya.'

'You're a dickhead, Dale.'

Then they hear *plop, plop* on the tin roof. Real goose poo rains down on them.

'Yuck!' Dale yells, wiping it from his face and hair.

Tomias rolls away, cracking up laughing. 'Stunned you!'

Honk! Honk! the geese answer. They fly away in formation, black in front of the lightness of the moon.

'C'mon, let's get that nest,' Dale says, serious now.

And they run to the edge of the roof and start searching through the branches of the mango tree for a greenants' nest to put in Miss Wilson's desk.

Mayali Language

ahnan – exclamation that means 'sooo cute'
bukulurl – full moon
djohboi – poor thing; dear thing
mabutj – chewing tobacco made from white ash and a tobacco plant
mandeuk – rain
yakki – exclamation of fear

Animals

bort – small perch or any small fish caught during Knock-'em-down time when they are fat and good to eat
djabbo – northern quoll (*Dasyurus halucatus*)
garrkanj – whistling kite (*Haliastur sphenurus*)
ginga – saltwater crocodile (*Crocodylus porosus*)
gomrdau *or* gornorrong – long-neck turtle (*Chelodina rugosa*)

Plants

djangeli – sand palm (*Livistona humilis*)

Non-Mayali words commonly used

gammon – pretend; not real life
humbug – be too demanding
myall – not properly trained; not educated; a person with no manners
shaggy – good, wicked, excellent, cool
subbie – understand; be familiar with
Toyoda – four-wheel-drive car
whatkind – exclamation of disbelief

The Author

Leonie Norrington was born in Darwin into a large Irish-Catholic family. She and her eight brothers and sisters became 'real bush kids'. They spent much of their childhood on a remote community in northern Australia, growing up among Aboriginal people who lived in the traditional way, and speaking Aboriginal English and Kriol.

After working at various jobs Leonie matriculated as a mature age student and went on to study journalism at Northern Territory University. Since then she has worked as a journalist and feature writer, published a gardening book (*Tropical Food Gardens*), and been a presenter for the popular ABC TV program *Gardening Australia*.

The Barrumbi Kids, her first novel for children, was published in 2002 to wide acclaim. She has also written a book for beginning readers, *Croc Bait*, which was published in the Omnibus Solo range in 2003.

Leonie and her husband live at Noonamah, near Darwin. They have three grown-up sons and one grandson.

